WISH, COME TRUE

For Nathan West
and all his doting relatives,
with love

WISH, COME TRUE

"You'll observe," said Great-Aunt Louise, "that I have redecorated the living room."

Joe hadn't observed. He didn't say anything. Meg said, "Oh."

"I repapered and repainted, and I even re-upholstered the couch," went on Great-Aunt Louise. She picked up the tiny couch and turned it this way and that so that Meg and Joe could see.

"Oh," said Joe. It wasn't very original, but it was all he could think of. "It's very pretty," said Meg, sounding bored.

Aunt Louise didn't seem to notice. She walked

around to the other side of the dollhouse and pointed into the kitchen.

"And I've got these copper-bottomed saucepans since you were here last," she added. "And let's see—oh, yes, the vases on the mantelpiece in the master bedroom."

She stepped back and surveyed the dollhouse proudly. Megan and Joe looked at each other. One of them ought to say something, but neither of them could think what. Neither of them said anything.

"Well," said Aunt Louise at last. "I suppose that's all. We'll go out now."

They went out of the room. Aunt Louise closed the door firmly behind them. Joe and Meg observed this. It meant "Don't ever go in this door unless I let you."

"I have it all in very fine condition," she said, smiling. "A Mr. Cooper is coming this week to look at it. He is organizing a touring exhibit of great dollhouses, and mine is one of the ones he is considering to take on the tour. It would be a great honor."

"Sure," said Joe.

"I guess so," said Meg.

They all three went into the living room, which hadn't been redecorated since 19-ought-4, Daddy said, and stood around aimlessly.

Oh, wow, thought Joe. I'm not going to be able to stand it. And Meg is going to do something awful, I bet. She's going to do it any minute now. How could Mother and Daddy *do* this?

What Joe's parents had done was go to France for three weeks. The first three weeks of summer vacation. They had just suddenly up and gone and left Megan and Joe with Great-Aunt Louise, because there wasn't anybody else who would take them.

"Mother, I'm warning you," Joe had said when they told him. "Something awful is going to happen. Something dire." *Dire* was a good word. He had just learned it. It meant "really terrible."

"Oh, don't be silly, Joe," Mother said. "Meg's not that babyish. She can stand three weeks. And she wouldn't spoil our trip. She knows how I've longed to go, and now that Daddy's getting his expenses paid, we can afford it finally."

She looked so happy Joe didn't say anything more. He didn't want to spoil things either. But anybody who thought Meg was going to spend three weeks with Great-Aunt Louise and not burst out somewhere had flipped. That's all there was to it, just flipped.

Meg had real talent for doing dire things. She could do them at a moment's notice. It didn't seem to be any trouble at all for her. Joe was always amazed. He would really have to work to do the things Meg did.

She could turn very white and go stiff all over, like somebody about to have a fit. Or she could turn pale blue and faint. Or she could turn pale green and throw up in a really spectacular fashion.

Mother and Daddy always said to ignore her when she did these things. But Joe couldn't ignore her. He sort of enjoyed seeing her do it, when there were no strangers around. And how could you ignore somebody who was throwing up all over your arithmetic book?

And he knew darn well Aunt Louise wasn't going to ignore Meg if any of those things happened in Aunt Louise's neat little house.

"Lunch time," said Aunt Louise. "You two sit here and I'll have it ready in just a minute."

She went out of the small, rather dark, old-fashioned living room, and Joe and Meg stared at each other. They didn't say anything for a while, until Meg said suddenly, "That dollhouse could be neat."

Joe was surprised. Meg didn't like playing with dolls any better than he did.

"How?" he asked, and then Aunt Louise called, "Lunch is ready," and they went through the small,

4

rather dark, old-fashioned dining room into the small, rather dark, old-fashioned kitchen to eat.

Joe was hungry, and lunch was great—pizza, really hot and gooey, and some kind of fruit drink. Aunt Louise's meals were always a surprise—there was nothing small or old-fashioned about them. She never ate a lot herself, but Joe and Megan guzzled.

After lunch they helped with the dishes, and then the children went back into the living room. Joe walked over to the window and looked out. He sighed. How could Mother and Daddy treat their own children like this? Three weeks in Aunt Louise's small, rather dark, old-fashioned city, in her small, rather dark, old-fashioned house . . . .

The rooms were all like the living room. Meg said her bedroom had a bed with a fringe of room around it. There was no place to play, scarcely any space to get dressed or undressed in.

The house had a little fringe of dismal grass and bushes around it. There was no park or playground for miles. They were right downtown.

Joe felt positively suffocated. He could hear the clock ticking and Aunt Louise moving around in the dining room, putting away plates and glasses. He heard the snick of the sideboard door when she was finished.

She put her head in through the living-room door.

"I'm going to take a nap now," she said. "I suppose you two are too old for naps these days?" Her voice was a little wistful, as though she hoped dreadfully they would say no, they weren't.

But Meg answered at once, "Way too old."

"Well, then, run outside and play," said Aunt Louise. "But don't cross the street, please. The traffic is so bad these days."

She yawned and went upstairs. Meg and Joe looked at each other again. "How do you mean, neat?" asked Joe again. But Meg didn't answer. She was on her way outdoors.

It was a clear day, a good day for swimming or picnicking or playing softball or just hanging around the playground, talking to other kids and teasing the real little ones. But here at Aunt Louise's—it might as well have been storming and hailing.

How could Mother and Daddy do this to two good kids like Meg and Joe? Two kids who hardly ever got into trouble—well, not bad trouble anyway. And weren't always asking for things like boxes of cereal with toy Martians or plastic dinosaurs in them.

All Mother said was, "Well, when I used to stay with Aunt Louise, I had a good time, a really great time."

"What did you do?" asked Joe.

"I can't remember," said Mother vaguely. "I just remember it was fun."

Joe stared at the patch of dismal grass and shrubs and wondered how in the world anybody could have a good time in a place like this.

They walked slowly all around the house. Under the dining-room windows they stopped and looked over into Mrs. Hollowell's yard. The only thing about Mrs. Hollowell's yard that was different from Aunt Louise's was a lump in the side yard. Meg and Joe puzzled over the heap of earth sitting up out of the rest of the ground like a small Indian mound.

"It's a grave, I bet," said Meg. "I bet she's got Mr. Hollowell buried under there."

"It's not big enough," said Joe. "Anyway, if Mr. Hollowell had died, the neighbors would have noticed."

Meg sighed. "I guess so," she admitted. She frowned at the sad-looking row of shrubbery between Aunt Louise's and Mrs. Hollowell's yards. "I'm going to go read a book." And she went.

It was easier for Meg, Joe thought sulkily. She could always read a book. She could read really well, and fast, and she liked it.

Reading was a chore for Joe. He had to spell out the words letter by letter, and then he didn't always get them right. One of the great things about school getting out was that he didn't have to read much. Just the books Mother made him read, sitting beside him and helping out. And Mother always picked pretty good books out of the library, but now she'd gone rushing off to France without bothering to go to the library and find anything for him. How could parents be so mean to a couple of good kids like Joe and Meg?

And besides reading, Megan had magic to think about. Joe didn't have anything to think about, not even being a National League pitcher, not the way Meg thought about magic.

When Meg had first said she wanted to be a magician, Mother had gone to the library and got a book for her. All about card tricks and making coins disappear. Meg had read it all. She gave Mother the book to take back to the library and Mother asked, "Do you want any more?"

"No, thanks," said Meg politely.

And later she had told Joe, "That's not the kind of magician I want to be at all. I want to be the kind that says, 'Behold! Your nursery fender is gold!'—and it's gold!"

"What's a nursery fender?" asked Joe.

"What's a nursery?" asked Meg.

"It's a place where you buy trees and plants and

things, I think," answered Joe. "I guess they have to have trucks and cars. So I guess you could call the fender on a nursery truck a nursery fender, if you wanted to."

It seemed like a kind of dumb thing to want to turn into gold. On the other hand that would be a lot of gold and a lot of money.

It wasn't money Meg wanted, though. What she wanted was to be able to make herself invisible or to turn chairs and tables into dogs and cats. Not to pretend to do them, but to do them in actual fact.

And what she wanted most was to turn herself into Joe. Joe thought she was nuts. But Meg wanted more than anything to be the oldest and get to stay up half an hour after the other one had gone to bed, and get to go to more movies, and not have to eat squash.

Of course, Joe didn't get out of eating squash because he was older. He got out of it because squash gave him hives. But there was no use trying to explain that to Meg.

Meg had bought a chemistry set and made all sorts of awful-looking and -smelling drinks, hoping they would give her magic powers. But she couldn't bring herself to swallow them. So she never knew whether they worked or not.

Still, she thought about it all the time. Driving

the hundred miles from where they lived to Aunt Louise's, she had thought and thought about it. And all Joe had had to think about was how much farther? And when do we eat? And now he didn't even have that to think about.

By and by Mr. Hollowell came out of his house and stared at Joe in an unfriendly way. Well, at least that proved he wasn't buried in the side yard, Joe thought. And after a while he went up to his room and spent the rest of the afternoon gloomily practicing spinning a Frisbee on the end of his finger.

He waited for something really dire to happen.

2

After supper the real horror dawned on Meg and Joe.

No TV. No nothing. Even some dumb game show was better than just sitting in Aunt Louise's tiny living room, staring at each other as the light grew dimmer and dimmer.

Aunt Louise didn't seem to mind. She sat in her small rocker busily knitting. Every now and then she glanced at the two children, and finally she must have realized that they were very bored.

"Would you like to play a game?" she asked. "I think I have a Chinese-checker board somewhere."

Meg frowned ferociously. She hated Chinese checkers. Joe didn't mind playing, but he wasn't going to play with Meg when she looked like that.

"No, thank you, Aunt Louise," he said politely. "I guess we'll just go read a book."

He could borrow one of Meg's. Sometimes her books were pretty good. He could ask her to help if he got stuck on a new word. He wouldn't like it, but he could do it. She always said, "What's the matter with you? That's a baby word." But he could put up with it, he'd been putting up with it for a long time.

"All right," agreed Aunt Louise, though she sounded a little doubtful. Did she know he had so much trouble reading? Joe wondered. He guessed so. Mother might have told her, though mostly Mother and Daddy only talked about it with Joe or with the eye doctor or with people at school, his teachers and people like that.

He got up and followed Meg upstairs.

"You got a book I might like?" he asked her. She pondered a minute. "I guess so," she answered finally. "There's a mystery I've finished. It was pretty good."

"Okay," he said glumly and went in her room while she looked through her stack of books and fished it out.

It looked thick. Meg knew he hated a long book. Still, he took it from her and went to his room, lay down on his bed and switched on the light. He read the first two sentences and then he got up and sat in a straight chair. Reading while he was lying down was even harder than reading while he was sitting up.

He was struggling with the third sentence when something made him look up. Aunt Louise was standing in his doorway.

"Joe," she said, "here's something which might interest you. I'd forgotten about it till just now."

She held a good-sized wooden box with a hasp lock. It was just a dull brown box, but right away something about it interested Joe. It looked old, and the hasp was sort of mysterious. He wondered if there was a padlock to go with it.

He jumped up and took the box from Aunt Louise's hands. It was so heavy he nearly dropped it.

"Careful," she said. "It's heavy."

"Yeah, I found out," Joe answered, wondering if it would have broken all his toes if he'd dropped it. Would Mother come home from France if he broke all his toes?

"This box belonged to my father," Aunt Louise explained. "He was your great-grandfather, a very well known and respected citizen of this town. He

13

was always interested in everything, and when he was a boy he collected things, all kinds of things. He put the best of his collections in this box and he gave it to me when I was quite grown-up, and I've kept it ever since. I don't know what all these keepsakes are—" she reached over and opened the box. A musty, earthy smell rose out of it— "but I'm sure some of them will entertain you. There are some arrowheads here. He's labeled each one with the date and place he found it. And here's a minié ball, a Civil War bullet, you know. And some odd stamps and coins."

As she poked these objects, her voice grew less certain, as though she wondered suddenly whether Joe cared about arrowheads. And he didn't really. What he liked was knowing that his own great-grandfather had collected and handled these things and written the neat words on the arrowheads.

"Gosh, they must all be awful old," he said suddenly.

"Of course," answered Aunt Louise. "The Civil War was over a hundred years ago. And the arrowheads would be even older."

And that wasn't what Joe had meant. He meant it had been a long time since his great-grandfather had been a boy and gathered up all these things. He felt as if the arrowheads hadn't really existed until someone had collected them. But he didn't know how to say this to Aunt Louise, so he just said, "Gosh," again.

"Well, I hope you enjoy looking at them," she said finally. "Just be careful. Don't lose any of them."

She went away. Joe put the box on the floor by his bed and moved the lamp from the bedside table onto the floor too.

The box was crowded with a helter-skelter of odds and ends. There was a brass cartridge case and something that looked like an animal tooth and an old sharpshooter's medal from the First World War. Had Great-Grandfather been a sharpshooter? Maybe so.

There were a couple of strange shells and some old, old marbles, made of real marble. He held one of these up and looked at it more closely. And then, he didn't know why, he thought of Megan. Meg was going to be mad if he didn't show her these things. He didn't want to. He wanted to keep them all to himself. But sooner or later she'd find out and she'd be mad. It was bad enough being shut up here at Aunt Louise's without having Meg mad at him. He heaved himself up off the floor and went and looked in Meg's door.

"What do you want?" she asked peevishly.

Good, thought Joe. Maybe she'll be in a bad mood and she won't come.

"I just thought you might want to look at these things Aunt Louise gave me," he said, trying not to sound too enthusiastic. But Meg sighed and laid her book down and followed him back to his room. He showed her the arrowheads and the old marbles and she was impressed.

"These are nice," she said, holding up a marble as Joe had done. "And they must be old, old, old."

"Old as the hills," he agreed. He had found a crocodile carved from black wood. "Look, Meg, its eyes move." Meg stared.

"That's sort of scary, like it was really alive," she said. "Maybe it really is. Crocodiles live a long time. Maybe that's a kind of petrified baby crocodile and it really is alive inside the wood."

Joe put it down quickly. "Don't be stupid," he said. "What's this?"

It was a big old English penny. "One penny," Joe spelled out laboriously. On the other side was a lot more wording, in a foreign language. Joe was horrified. Why would English people want a lot of hard-to-read foreign words on their money?

"I wonder why they made them so big?" he asked. "If you wanted to buy something that cost a lot of pennies, you'd have to take them in a wheelbarrow or something."

"What's this?" asked Meg. She held up a dark, knobbly metal hoop.

16

"A metal washer, I guess," Joe answered, looking at it briefly. He didn't think it was interesting. He went on looking at the arrowheads, but Meg studied the tarnished circle carefully.

"I think it's a ring," she announced at last. "A magic ring, from deep inside the earth. It has great powers."

"Magic!" cried Joe. "That's all you think about. You're nuts. It's just an old washer."

"It's a magic ring," said Meg impressively.

"Ah, go on," responded Joe. "What can it do, then?"

"It can make me be you," replied Meg.

Meg was off her rocker, Joe thought. He ought to be the one who wanted to change, so he could read like a flash of lightning and be the one who got good grades in school and always had enough to think about so he wasn't bored.

And could do dire things, like flinging the world's fiercest tantrums.

"Well, it can't," he said shortly. Meg's eyes widened. "Yes, it can," she stated flatly. "It already has."

Joe considered. "No, it hasn't," he said. "I'm still me and not you."

"No, we've changed places," Meg told him, sounding smug.

"No, we haven't," argued Joe. "I'm still me."

"How can you tell we haven't?" asked Meg. "If I'm you, I would feel like you and you'd feel like me, wouldn't you? It wouldn't do me any good to be you if I was going to feel like me, would it?"

Joe was confused. "Well, anyway, that thing isn't any of your old magic. It's just something plumbers use," he growled. He picked up one of the minié balls. "I wonder what these are made out of?" he went on. "Is it lead? I guess it must be. They're funny-looking, aren't they?"

"It *is* magic," Meg insisted. "I can feel it in my bones." She stopped and sat very still, feeling her bones. Joe's bones didn't feel anything except a bruised place on his shin where he'd fallen over a suitcase.

"Oh, the foot bone's connected to the anklebone," he sang softly. "The anklebone's connected—"

"Shut up," snapped Meg. "Listen, Joe, if this is a magic ring it can do lots of great things. It could make us little so we could go in Aunt Louise's dollhouse. It could make us so we could see through walls and catch bank robbers and murderers and things."

"I don't want to catch murderers and bank robbers," Joe answered promptly. "That's what the police are for. And they know how to do it better than we do. We'd just get shot or stabbed if we tried."

18

He didn't say anything about being made small enough to go in Aunt Louise's dollhouse. That might be neat. Provided the ring could make them big again. He wondered for a minute if he really *was* Meg.

"Well, I'm going to find out what it can do," said Meg. "I think it can do lots of things. And if you don't want to do lots of magic, you don't have to."

"Time for your baths," said Aunt Louise. Joe wondered if she had been standing in the doorway very long and if she'd heard what Meg said and if she was going to have his sister taken away to the funny farm. If she had heard, she didn't say anything.

"I hope you're enjoying my father's mementos," she went on. "Some of the things are really very nice. I wish I knew more about them."

"What about this?" asked Meg, holding up the "magic ring." "Do you know what this is, Aunt Louise?"

Aunt Louise inspected it. "No, I don't," she answered finally. "But it doesn't seem terribly interesting. I suppose my father must have had some reason for saving it, however. Maybe it had some private meaning for him."

Megan looked discontented. They gathered up all the things and put them back in the box. Joe was almost sure the "magic ring" hadn't gone back in, but he didn't ask about it.

Meg had her bath and went off to bed, and then it was Joe's turn. He took his bath and washed out the tub and dragged on his pajamas, and all the while he was thinking about that ring. He wished he wouldn't.

It was dumb. But was he really Meg? Was Meg right and he wouldn't notice the change? If he was Meg at least he ought to be able to read fast. Twice in the night he got up and turned on the light and tried reading his book. But he hadn't changed. He still had to sound out every word a slow letter at a time. It was still harder than doing thirty push-ups. He shut the book and at last went to sleep.

3

At breakfast Meg looked white and tense.

"Do you feel well, Megan?" asked Aunt Louise. "Did you sleep well? You don't think you're coming down with something, do you?"

"I'm fine, Aunt Louise," answered Megan with a tiny smile. "I slept okay."

Joe wondered why she didn't say she was having appendicitis and Mother and Daddy should come right home instead of running around France leaving their helpless children to suffer. Well, he knew why she didn't say that, and he knew why she looked so funny. She and her bones were concentrating on

21

that ring. It was going to be a magic ring if it killed Meg.

After the breakfast dishes were done she beckoned him silently up the stairs to her room. She shut the door. She was so pale the freckles on her nose were almost black in contrast to the rest of her skin. She sort of scared Joe.

"You sure you're not sick or something?" he asked.

"Shhh," she answered. "Aunt Louise mustn't hear. Listen, Joe, this ring is magic, real magic. I know it is. And if we can find out how it works—" she broke off.

"I guess you just put it on and wish," he said slowly.

"You must think I'm stupid," she yelled. "That was the first thing I tried!"

She put her hand over her mouth and looked alarmed. Fortunately a huge moving van was passing the house at that moment, so it wasn't likely Aunt Louise heard.

"I think you have to say some magic words," she went on after they had waited a minute.

"Hocus-pocus," said Joe helpfully. "Alleykazam! Open sesame!"

Meg gave him a withering look. She held out her hand with the ring lying, dark and lumpy and dull-looking, in her palm.

"I think the words are printed or carved or something inside," she told him. "Inside the ring. See if you can read them."

Joe glared at her. She was making fun of him. She knew he couldn't read well. But then he saw she wasn't making fun. She really wanted him to try to figure out what was written on the inside of the ring. He took it from her and stared at the little worn, scratchy marks. He couldn't make out a single letter.

"I expect it says 'Patent Pending,'" he said finally. "It says that on a lot of things."

Meg looked really ferocious.

"Maybe it says 'Post No Bills,'" he added hastily. "I mean, 'Private Property.' Or 'This Side Up.' Look, Meg, I can't read it. It's not my fault."

He handed the ring back, and she took it sulkily and rubbed it on her shirt sleeve. It stayed as black and tarnished as ever.

"It is magic," she insisted. "I *know* it is. And it *can* grant wishes."

She slipped it on her finger. "I wish to be little, I wish to be little, I wish to be little," she chanted on and on.

She went on chanting even after she really was little. Her voice got little too. Joe had been looking out the window and not paying much attention. It was only when he could barely hear her that he turned around to see what was the matter—and couldn't find her.

"Meg?" he said, feeling a little scared.

"Here I am!" she yelled. And there she was, by the toe of his tennis shoe. And then he really was scared. He didn't like having real magic happen. He didn't like having a sister who was no bigger than a lightning bug. And suppose she couldn't get back to her real size again? And suppose he stepped on her?

Meg wasn't scared. She was whirling around and around singing, "I can do real magic! I can do real magic!" Joe crouched on his hands and knees, trying not to step on her. He wished she wouldn't dance around so.

"How did you do it?" he asked in a whisper. He was afraid to speak in his normal voice for fear he might blow her away.

Meg stopped dancing. "I don't know," she answered. "I just said, 'I wish to be little,' over and over, till it happened."

"It must be the number of times you say it," Joe whispered. "Three's a magic number, isn't it?"

"It was more than three," Meg answered. "Seven is a magic number. Maybe seven."

"Well, whatever it was, make yourself big again," said Joe. "You give me the creeps. And Aunt Louise

24

is around somewhere. And I'm sure not going to tell her what happened to you."

"Okay," said Meg. She held up her quarter-inch-long hand with the ring still on it and chanted over and over, "I wish to be big, I wish to be big, I wish to be big. . . ."

"That's seventeen times," said Joe at last. "It isn't going to work. You're going to have to live in a cricket cage."

Now Meg did look a little worried.

"Rats, I wish I'd counted," she said. She pulled the reddish hair over her left ear the way she always did when she was upset.

"Maybe you were doing something else at the same time, like standing on your left foot," Joe suggested.

"No, I wasn't," snapped Meg. "I was just standing here saying that and rub—" Her eyes grew wide. "—rubbing the ring from right to left. That's magic."

"Well, try that, for pete's sake," cried Joe. "And hurry!"

Meg's fingers, as small as ants' legs, rubbed the ring while she said over and over, "I wish to be big, I wish to be big."

She was big all right. Her head cracked the ceiling and her bony, blue-jeaned knees sent Joe flying across the bed.

"Can't you do anything right?" he muttered, and then hoped she didn't hear him. She was big enough to step on him now. And she probably would if she got really mad.

"Oh, oh, oh, my head," moaned Meg, squeezed between the bed and the closet door. "Oh, ouch!"

"Meg, do something quick," begged Joe. "You're making an awful racket. Aunt Louise is going to come in here any minute."

The thought of Aunt Louise finding Meg like this was really dire. At least when she was so little he could have hidden her for a while till he thought of something.

"It was nine times," said Meg from up near the light fixture. "I counted. Three is a magic number, so nine is three times as magic because it's three times three."

"Okay, I know, I know," said Joe. "But hurry, would you?"

"What'll I say?" moaned Meg. "I can't say, 'I wish to be big,' or 'I wish to be little.' Oh, I know!"

With some difficulty she got her hands together and began to rub the ring. "I wish to be my right size again," she chanted nine times. And there she was. Only she wasn't pale any more, her cheeks were red with excitement and there was a small cobweb in her hair.

"Oh, Joe, I can do magic, real magic!" she yelled.

"Well, turn the nursery fender to gold," said Joe somewhat bitterly. "We'll sell it and take the money and go to France. You keep making so much racket Aunt Louise isn't going to let us stay here much longer anyway. She's going to send us to the juvenile detention home."

He didn't point out that Megan hadn't done any magic. Only the ring had done magic. Still, she had found out how to use it, which was more than he had done. What's more, she was probably going to turn him into a pumpkin if he mentioned it.

"I don't think the ring will do things like turning stuff to gold," said Megan.

"Well, try," urged Joe. He didn't like to think that ring had any sort of powers, but as long as it did—and it certainly seemed to—it might as well make itself useful.

Meg looked around the room. Her eye lit on the book she had been reading. "That's plenty big," she told him. "A gold book would be worth tons of money."

"Okay, okay," said Joe impatiently. "Just get on with it, would you?"

Meg rubbed the ring on her left middle finger and softly repeated nine times, "I wish this book to be turned to gold. . . ."

The book obstinately remained a library book. Not even the letters of the title turned to gold. Meg looked angry, and Joe looked sad.

"I didn't think it was that kind of magic," she said at last. "The only thing the ring can do is make us things, like little or big or able to fly or things like that."

It was just as well, Joe thought. He bet people wouldn't buy a solid gold book anyway. But he was already a pretty good pitcher and the ring could make him the best. And when he got home . . . . He was still dreaming about no-hitters and what he was going to say to Catfish Hunter when they met, when Meg said, "Of course, I really don't know whether it will work on you either. Or whether you can make it work."

Joe was startled. He didn't want to make it work. Meg was the one who wanted to do magic, not him. He didn't mind her making him the best pitcher in the world, but he didn't want to fiddle around with magic himself.

Still, he took the ring when she gave it to him and put it on. He didn't want Meg to think he was afraid.

"You rub it this way," she instructed. "And say nine times, 'I wish to be six feet tall.'"

Halfheartedly Joe did as she told him to. Nothing

happened. So it really was Meg who was magic, and the ring only worked for her.

"Here, give it back," she said quickly, and he was glad to hand it over. She slipped the ring back on her finger and repeated nine times, "I wish Joe to be six feet tall."

He had a strange sensation, and then he was looking down at Meg and she was reeling around the room, laughing and laughing.

4

Joe looked down at his long length and was horrified. He didn't think it was a bit funny. The ring had made him six feet tall all right, but it hadn't troubled to make him any bigger around than he had been before. He was weird. He looked like he might break any minute.

"Hey, Meg, cut it out," he yelled. "Make me back like I was. I feel like a goalpost."

Meg just went on giggling.

"Come on, Meg," he begged. "I might get stuck this way. How would you like having a brother who looked like this forever and ever?"

And after a while Meg managed to calm down and wish him back to his old height and shape.

"Oh, boy," he said. "I'm going to eat all the pies and doughnuts I can get my hands on. I don't ever want to be that skinny again. Wow, I was scared my legs were going to snap in two."

"You know something funny?" Meg asked. "The magic works on your clothes too. I guess that's lucky. But I wish you'd taken off your jeans and we could have kept them like that. They looked like —like—" She began to laugh again. And then suddenly she said, "You remember how I said Aunt Louise's dollhouse could be a lot of fun? Well, what I meant was if we could get little and go inside it. And we can! Oh, we really can!"

Joe thought it might be pretty neat.

"But we're not even supposed to go in the room with it," he pointed out. "You know we're not."

"Things like that don't count if you're magicked," said Meg airily. "If you're magicked you're already breaking all the rules anyway. You might as well break a few more. It hardly counts because if you're magicked you're not really real. And anyway, we won't hurt the dollhouse."

Maybe she was right. Joe felt uneasy about the whole thing. But Meg was so pleased with herself and he was so pleased that she wasn't going to do something dire, at least for a while, that he didn't say anything else.

They spent the rest of the morning experimenting with the ring. The ring was fussy. It would not make them float like balloons. Joe thought that was probably a good thing. People who got wings or floated or otherwise were able to bump around on the ceiling always got stuck somewhere and had to be rescued and then had to think of some explanation of why they were where they were. Joe wasn't good at explaining things, not even simple things, like how he managed to drop his watch into the spaghetti in the school cafeteria.

The ring would not make them invisible. Meg was disappointed. She tried saying, "I wish to be invisible," eighty-one times, because if nine was three times as magic as three, eighty-one was nine times more magic than nine.

Listening to her say it and marking the number of times on a piece of paper about drove Joe up the wall. And when she suggested trying eighty-one times eighty-one, he figured out that was 6,561 times.

"You'll be here till next year doing that," he told her. "Besides, you'd probably rub the ring down to nothing."

So she didn't try.

The ring would not make them able to walk through walls. Meg got another bump on her head finding that out. It did make Joe so strong he could pick up the end of Meg's bed with his little finger and it gave Meg black hair, which she had always wanted and which looked very peculiar on her. Meg undid all these things before lunch.

And while they were clearing up the lunch things, Aunt Louise said, "Oh, I am afraid you children are terribly bored here." She polished the forks with silver polish, as she did after every meal. "And now I must go out for a while, to have my hair cut and buy a few things. Would you like to go to a movie this afternoon? I could take you there and then pick you up afterward. I mean, come for you. We'd have to ride the bus, of course."

Joe and Megan got a newspaper and looked to see what was on at the movies. A dog story, which was sure to be sad and make Meg cry buckets, really sob and wail, the way she always did and embarrassed Joe within an inch of his life; and a movie about an earthquake which would be the same boring old earthquake they had both seen a thousand times on TV.

"I guess we'll just stay home, Aunt Louise," said Meg, trying to sound as though she wasn't dying to get back upstairs and do something with that ring.

"Are you sure?" asked Aunt Louise. "There's a new playground about ten blocks away. But I really feel the supervision there is not the best. I shouldn't want you to have an accident or anything like that. I would feel very badly indeed, as I am responsible for your welfare."

"It's okay," said Joe. "We'll be all right here. We don't mind staying home."

Actually he did mind a lot. He didn't feel at all sure he was the kind of person who ought to get mixed up with magic. Meg was that kind of person maybe, but he wasn't. Still, that old ring might keep something dire from happening. And it had certainly kept them from being bored all morning.

When Aunt Louise had gone to catch her bus, Meg did a dance of triumph in the little dark living room. She was grinning from ear to ear.

"Now's the time," she said breathlessly. "Now's the time, Joe. While she's gone, we can get in the dollhouse!"

Joe wished earnestly that he had gone to see that earthquake. And then he had a happy thought.

"How?" he asked. "It's up on a table. If we're little enough to get in it, we can't climb the table. And your dumb old ring can't make us weightless or anything really good like that."

Meg turned pale. "Don't say such awful, horrible things!" she whispered. "It might hear you, and

34

then if it got its feelings hurt, it wouldn't do anything at all."

"For crying out loud," began Joe, and then he remembered about dire things happening and how much Meg had wanted the ring to be magic. And about how he was going to get magicked into being the world's best pitcher. So he shut up. "Well, all right, I didn't mean it. It's a great ring. But you still haven't said how we're going to get in that dollhouse."

"Hush," said Meg. "I'm thinking." She thought a long time. Joe thought too but he didn't have an idea and if he had he wouldn't have mentioned it. Maybe.

"If it could work on things, I could turn a piece of paper into a magic carpet," she said. "I'd say, 'Take us to the dollhouse living room—' and there we'd be."

She stopped and looked startled, and then she slipped on the ring and began to rub it.

"I wish Joe and me to be small enough to get in the dollhouse and I wish us to be there," she said nine times, and Joe felt a whooshing of air and a slight dizzy sensation.

They were there. It was as simple as that. They were in the dollhouse living room and they were exactly the right size.

"Neat-o," said Joe in grudging admiration.

The dollhouse living room was nice. It was much lighter and prettier than Aunt Louise's real living room. Joe walked around, stepping carefully, as he was not certain he didn't weigh as much as he used to when he was big.

"Look at the clock on the mantelpiece," he said. "It even tells the right time."

"I told you the ring could do it," chortled Meg. "I expect it can do anything if you just knew the right way to ask it. Oh, great!"

They went all over the living room and dining room and kitchen. By and by it dawned on Joe that this was pretty dull. The point of all those little things was that they were little and people were big. When you were the right size to sit in a three-inch chair it was just a chair, and you and it might as well be back in Aunt Louise's dining room.

Even the eggbeater that really worked in the kitchen didn't seem to him so very wonderful. Though he did admire those little bitty screws. Had a watchmaker made it? A lot of the things looked as though they'd been made—well, by fairies or something pretty weird. Aunt Louise made a lot of them herself. She must be smarter than Joe had thought.

"Let's go upstairs," suggested Meg.

"Do you think we can?" asked Joe. "The steps might break."

"Oh, don't be dumb," she snapped. "We're mag-icked, remember?"

They went upstairs. Even Megan was a little cau-tious, and Joe was scared. But nothing happened. The little flight of steps didn't even creak.

Upstairs was just the same, only bedrooms were even less exciting to stare at than kitchens. Joe was just about to tell Megan he wanted out when there was a sound of voices in the hall. And then foot-steps and the doorknob turning and oh, good grief! Aunt Louise!

And somebody else, a man. Mr. Cooper, who was going to exhibit dollhouses.

Joe was frozen. He couldn't move. Meg pushed him.

"Under the bed, dumbbell. Under the bed!" she whispered.

He hit his shin again getting under the bed. Aunt Louise's voice sounded quite close.

"I don't know how I could have done such a thing, just completely forgotten you were coming," she said a little breathlessly. "I was coming out of the dime store when I remembered. Such a very stupid thing! I took a taxi at once and arrived not two minutes before you drove up. If you don't mind, I'll go put these bags down and call the hairdresser. You look at the house. I won't be a second."

She went away. Beside him Joe could hear Megan

whispering, "I wish Joe and me to be back in my room I wish Joe and me . . . ." She was never going to get to nine, never.

Mr. Cooper's big finger touched the edge of the bedspread and began to pull it up. . . .

5

Joe was scared. He was really shaking. It was like a horror movie, only a lot worse. In a minute Mr. Cooper was going to lift up the whole bed and there they'd be and what would happen then?

He stared at the enormous, clean pink fingertip reaching toward him, and he knew he was inching away and his feet were probably poking out on the other side.

"Hic!" said Meg. "Hic! Hic!"

He glared at her in the gloom of under the bed. She had the hiccups! Meg was the only person in the world who would get hiccups from being scared.

Being scared cured other people of the hiccups.

Mr. Cooper's fingertip withdrew.

"Oh, the lovely little vases," he murmured.

"Hold your breath!" whispered Joe fiercely to Meg.

"Hic!" said Meg.

"Bite a lemon, do something," begged Joe silently.

"Hic!" said Meg.

"Really remarkable," breathed Mr. Cooper. "Unbelievable workmanship."

"I wish Joe and I were our right size—hic!—and back in my room," whispered Meg. "Oh, I'll have to start over. Hic! I've lost count."

"Just keep on, you've got to get to nine sometime or other. And hurry, would you?" said Joe. "And keep it down."

He saw the shadow of Mr. Cooper's hand approaching the bed once more.

"Eyelet lace," said Mr. Cooper.

"Hic! Back in my room," whispered Meg, and they were.

Joe sat down on the bed. If he had known how to faint, he would have done it. He was trembling all over.

"That was close," he said in a quavering voice.

"Oh, I expect it would have been all right if he'd

seen us," answered Meg. "He'd have thought we were dolls if we hadn't moved, I suppose."

"I couldn't help moving," Joe told her. "I was shaking all over, I was so scared. I don't like magic. As far as I'm concerned you can forget the whole thing."

At supper Aunt Louise was tremendously pleased and excited.

"Mr. Cooper thought it was among the finest he'd seen of the simpler dollhouses," she told them. "Oh, he admired everything. He said that when he first looked in, it seemed so real he could almost believe he heard little voices."

"Great," said Joe, hearing the little voices in his mind's ear. "Is he going to exhibit it?"

"I think so," she answered. "Although there are many much finer ones around the country, I'm sure."

She looked modest but she was really proud, Joe knew. He thought about that eggbeater.

Megan was silent. She was sulking because the dollhouse had been sort of a flop and Joe had said he didn't want anything more to do with that magic stuff. He didn't know how he was going to get out of it without causing something dire to happen. But he was going to. Meg could turn purple with blue spots and lose all her hair, he wasn't going to be that scared again.

And the next day he thought he wasn't going to have to, at least for a while. Because in the morning an old friend of Aunt Louise's called and invited them all to visit her "in the country."

"You'll like Pat," Aunt Louise assured them. "And she lives in a really nice place."

Joe and Meg liked Pat. She was a big woman and she wore blue jeans and a T-shirt that said "Hurray for Trees" across its front. She came for them in her car. But the "country" was a disappointment. No cows, no fields of beans or corn, no barns. Just trees and grasses and small houses with flower beds.

But there was a lake! Not big, but big enough, with reeds and cattails around the edges and a rowboat pulled up among the reeds with the oars lying inside.

"That's my boat," said Pat. "I'll take you for a row before lunch."

Aunt Louise stayed behind. Pat rowed out over the water, clear water, so that they could look down and see the bottom, part sand, part rock. Little schools of minnows flashed away from the oars, a redwing blackbird sang, and a bigger bird started up out of the reeds as they passed and skittered over the water's surface as though it was a solid thing under the bird's feet.

"That's a coot," said Pat. "Stays here all summer. Now I'll show you something really good."

She rowed toward the far end of the lake and then she pulled up the oars and let the boat rock along.

"Over there," she said. And there, against the sandy bottom, six enormous fish lay looking as though they were fast asleep. Huge and gray and still, motionless in the motionless water.

"Carp," said Pat. "Must be twelve, fifteen years old. Maybe older."

"Doesn't anybody ever try to catch them?" asked Joe.

"They'd better not," said Pat. "They're sort of pets around here."

She slipped the oars back into the water, and the fish swam lazily away toward the shelter of the reeds.

"What about winter?" asked Meg. "Don't they get frozen?"

"No," Pat answered. "It hardly ever gets cold enough to freeze the lake all the way across. Anyway, fishes manage somehow. I don't know much about things like that, but I think they sort of slow down a lot. They don't need much air or food, like bears when they hibernate."

Joe was glad he wasn't a fish. He liked needing a lot to eat, so at lunch he had three helpings of potato salad.

They ate on the porch, and Pat's house was really

near the lake. They could watch the sun and the wind on the water and hear the redwing blackbird call. It was a lot more fun than being in a dollhouse, Joe thought.

After lunch Meg said, "Could we go play by the lake?"

"Sure," Pat said.

"Could we swim?" asked Joe.

They hadn't brought bathing suits, but they could swim in their shorts. They'd done it before.

"I'm sorry," Pat answered. "No swimming allowed without a lifeguard, and he doesn't come till three this afternoon. He has some other job he goes to on Thursday."

Joe and Meg looked at each other. Why hadn't Pat asked them for Friday then? And it was silly, they knew how to swim and all about the buddy system and the things not to do.

"You could wade," said Aunt Louise suddenly. "But be very careful."

Wading was better than nothing, Joe told Meg. The water was cool and they could see a red-spotted newt walking slowly away from them, and whirligig beetles spun around their knees.

"It would be nice to wade on out and see those big fish," said Meg.

"You couldn't," said Joe. "You'd float and that's the same as swimming, I guess."

Meg looked thoughtful. She put her hand in her pocket and brought out the ring.

"Now wait a minute," cried Joe. "I already said forget it. I don't want to be magicked any more."

"Okay," Meg answered. "I'll just magic me."

Joe glared at her. "What are you going to do?" he asked reluctantly.

"I'm going to make it so I can walk underwater and go see those carp," she said calmly. "I'll still be wading, I'll just be wading underwater."

"Well, you'll have to make it so you can breathe and see," he pointed out.

"And breathe and see," she agreed. She slipped on the ring.

"Oh, all right, me too," Joe said. He might as well. If Meg got in trouble he'd be in trouble, even if he wasn't magicked, because that's the way things worked.

"I wish that Joe and I could walk and breathe and see underwater," recited Meg nine times, rubbing the ring.

"I bet it won't do it," Joe muttered.

Meg walked straight out toward the middle of the lake, and after a second he followed. It was weird. He could feel the water, cool and pleasant, pressing against his legs, but at the same time he couldn't feel it. It was more like walking against a wind than in water. And even when the level got up to his

45

chest he could put his feet down firmly on the bottom. He wasn't almost on tiptoes the way he would be ordinarily if he had walked into water that deep.

Meg went on. She was in up to her nose, to the top of her head. Had she drowned? No, he could see her walking on, moving slowly through the clear water.

He held his breath and shut his eyes and went forward. But that was really dumb. He couldn't keep it up very long. He opened his eyes and found that again he knew the water was there, but he didn't truly feel it. And he could see perfectly.

He took a tiny breath—and there was no choking or burbling or water in his nose and throat, just air. He'd always heard there was a lot of air in water, and he guessed the ring had figured some way to filter the air out for them. He took another breath and another, each time expecting to find water in his lungs, and each time he was surprised and glad when he didn't.

Meg turned around. She grinned and said something. He heard a low, growly sound and saw a lot of bubbles, but they'd forgotten about talking, and the ring evidently arranged nothing on its own. It was what their mother called literal-minded.

But it didn't matter. He knew what Meg was saying, and she was right. This was great.

The minnows swam by and slipped their shining bodies in and out between Meg and Joe. Meg's reddish brown hair was full of silver bubbles. It made her almost pretty, Joe thought.

He walked toward her, and a water beetle swam slowly by, right in front of him. Joe was glad he wasn't dollhouse size any more. That beetle looked like it could eat a couple of dollhouse-sized children and still have room for dessert.

He wished they could find the carp. Over there was a dark something, and he went toward it, but it was only a big rock. He looked around, and the water wavered here and there and broke into rainbows. Overhead was the bright silver sheet of reflected sunlight. There were the reeds and cattails, like a jungle with no top, ending right at the water's glittering surface. The rainbow colors chased in and out and among the reeds as the minnows dashed here and there.

It was pretty neat, thought Joe. It was like nothing he'd ever seen or heard of before. The bad thing about it was, he was never going to be able to tell anybody else about it, not ever in a million years. His dad would like hearing about it, and his mother too. But they wouldn't believe a word of it, that Joe and Meg had walked along the bottom of a lake as though it was a path in the woods. That they'd seen these things with their bare eyes and not had to use goggles or flippers or an oxygen tank or anything.

The big dark something Joe had thought was a rock suddenly put out a nose and a tail and four stubby legs and walked slowly away. A turtle! Meg pinched him and pointed at it. He rubbed his arm and growled at her. Meg never poked you or said, "Hey, look!" She pinched, and he didn't think it was nice.

He moved away so she wouldn't do it again, but she followed and pinched again anyway. She gestured with her hands, but he couldn't understand what she meant, so she showed him. Carefully she lay down and stretched full length on the pebbly, sandy floor.

That was a pretty good idea, Joe thought. They could lie there and look up and things wouldn't notice them so much as when they were standing. The carp just might come swimming over.

He lay down beside her and stared up and waited. They didn't wait long. There was a terrific swirl of water, billions of bubbles, a kicking, thrashing body, and the next thing Joe knew he was being hauled up onto the bank and a hoarse voice shouted, "Help! Help! Need help for two drowned people!"

6

There hadn't been anyone in sight when Joe and Meg walked out into the lake. Joe had checked to be sure. But now people came running from all directions, a lot of kids that you would have thought would be outdoors on a nice day like this, several frightened-looking women, some dogs, a postman and a fat man in green shorts and a brightly flowered shirt who was yelling, "Mouth-to-mouth resuscitation! Mouth-to-mouth resuscitation!" over and over.

Meg struggled out of their rescuer's arms. Joe had already been dropped on the grass, where he lay without moving. He was scared again.

"Mouth-to-mouth resuscitation!" bellowed the fat man.

"We aren't drowned!" cried Meg, glaring around. "We aren't drowned, for pete's sake!"

The young man who had dragged them out of the water looked at her in astonishment.

"What happened?" asked one of the frightened-looking mothers.

"I waded out a little, and Joe came after me," explained Meg truthfully just as the young man said, "They was laying on the bottom of the lake. Right flat on the bottom."

"Mouth-to-mouth resuscitation, that's the ticket!" cried the fat man.

Joe could see Meg beginning to turn a little green at the mere thought. He didn't like the idea too much himself.

"Well, they should be ashamed," put in another woman. "Playing a trick like that. And there's no swimming allowed on Thursdays anyhow."

"On the bottom of the lake," stated the young man again. "They sure looked drowned to me."

Everyone stared accusingly at Meg and Joe. Pat stepped up.

"On the bottom of the lake!" she repeated. "Bill, these children are hardly even damp."

It was true. Evidently, in order that they could

breathe and see, the ring had somehow protected Meg and Joe from the water. Their hair and clothes were only as wet as they would have got during some rather splashy wading.

"Well, they was there," said Bill stubbornly. "I saw 'em as soon as I got out of the car."

"We weren't drowning," Meg said in an equally stubborn tone.

The women frowned at them, the kids and dogs began to drift away, the fat man said once more, "Mouth-to-mouth resuscitation."

"Oh, dear," said Aunt Louise. "I'm sorry you were put to so much trouble. Can we—I mean—what about some dry clothes?"

"I live right over there," said Bill.

"Well, we do appreciate it, of course," said Pat. "If the children had really been in trouble, we'd have been lucky you were here. Come in the house and have a Coke and some cookies."

"No, thanks," said Bill a little sulkily. "I've got to get home."

"Well, thank you very much anyway," said Aunt Louise and shook his hand with a hand that surely had a five-dollar bill in it.

Meg, Joe, Pat and Aunt Louise walked back to Pat's house, leaving the women still looking provoked and Bill explaining again to the fat man that "those kids was laying flat on the bottom of the lake."

"Bill Anderson's a nice boy, but he's not too bright," said Pat.

"I expect the sun on the lake made some strange reflection," said Aunt Louise. "I'm sure he was certain the children were underwater. And the sun is certainly brilliant."

She gave Meg and Joe a grave look, and Meg shoved her hand hastily into the pocket of her shorts.

On the drive home the children were very quiet, and Pat and Aunt Louise talked about the difficulty of buying really comfortable shoes.

No more magic, Joe told himself once more. Not ever. That's a promise.

"Not ever," he told Meg later. "No more ring."

"That was neat underwater," she pointed out.

"Yeah," he admitted. It had been neat. He'd liked it a lot. "But suppose *two* people had seen us lying there? Even Pat and Aunt Louise would have had to believe *two* people. And those others were really mad at us for scaring them. They thought we'd done it on purpose, for a joke or something. And Aunt Louise didn't like it."

Meg pulled her hair.

"No more ring," he repeated.

"Well, I still can use it," she replied. "I can be magicked all by myself."

In a way Joe was sorry. After all, she had wanted so much to do real magic. And now she could do it. And it must be more fun to do magic with somebody to see than to have to do it all by yourself with nobody to show off to.

But he wasn't going to have anything more to do with it. Both times he'd let himself get talked into it, he'd ended up being scared out of his skull and close to being in some sort of trouble—he didn't know what. But trouble.

"What'll you do all by yourself?" he asked. Maybe it would be kind to let her talk about it anyway.

"I'll—I'll turn myself into a Martian," said Meg and grinned.

"You'd better not," said Joe.

"Why not?" she asked.

"I expect Martians are just blobs," said Joe. "They don't have hands. If you don't have hands, how are you going to rub the ring and turn yourself back?"

Meg thought a minute. "You're a wet blanket," she said at last and flounced out of the room.

Next morning Aunt Louise decided to let them go to the new playground, even though it was ten blocks away and even though she was worried about the supervision.

"Would you like me to go with you?" she asked

nervously. Joe didn't know whether she was afraid they'd say yes or no.

"We'll find it all right," Meg told her.

"And we'll cross at the corners, with the lights," Joe added.

"Don't worry, Aunt Louise," Meg said. "We'll be careful. We don't have a very good supervisor at our playground at home and we never get hurt or anything." Which wasn't really true. The supervisors were great, and last year Meg had fallen off a trapeze and Joe had sprained his ankle sliding into second base.

"Oh, I'm an old fuddy-duddy," said Aunt Louise. "You're quite right, You're old enough to be responsible for yourselves. Run along and have a good time. But do be careful crossing streets."

On the way Joe thought about asking Meg to magic him into being a great pitcher. But then he decided it wasn't worth the trouble it would no doubt get him into. The ring would probably make his fast balls so fast they would burst into flame and go up in smoke. Anyway, he was pretty good without any old ring to help.

And then, when they got to the playground, he discovered he needn't have worried. The playground was small, and there really wasn't room for a decent ball game. And the kids there were all small, just little kids.

Joe and Meg wandered around and climbed on the parallel bars and finally got a chance at the two trapezes. But after a while the supervisor came over and asked if they would mind letting the little ones have the trapezes back.

"They're not meant for people as big as you—the trapezes I mean," she said apologetically. And they really weren't. When Joe hung by his knees his head almost touched the ground.

Meg went to stand in line and wait for her turn on the slide, but Joe had outgrown slides a long time ago.

Joe wandered around and watched the smallest kids swinging from the trapezes. He thought maybe little kids had more fun than big kids. The ones on the trapezes were all shouting and giggling about nothing.

Some little girls were playing jacks near the jungle gym. They giggled and shouted too. They bounced the ball all over the place, and one of them finally grabbed all the jacks and stuffed them in her pocket. They all seemed to think this was the funniest thing yet, and yelled with laughter.

Joe walked away. If the kids around here didn't

play baseball any better than they played jacks, he was glad not to play.

After a while he and Meg started back to Aunt Louise's. They crossed carefully at all the corners. Joe had never been so bored in his life.

If things didn't get better soon, he might do something dire himself. Well, he wouldn't. However, Meg probably would. And he really couldn't say he'd blame her. He looked at her to see if she was turning green or blue or anything.

But she wasn't. She was walking along the dull, hot sidewalk in front of the neat, dull buildings and houses, and she looked rather pleased with herself.

"What we need," she said finally, "is some money. And I think I know how to get it."

7

"What do we need money for?" asked Joe.

"Everybody needs money," pointed out Meg.

"Sure," Joe agreed. "But right now there's not much we could do with it if we had it. We got enough to go to the movies or buy ice cream and stuff like that."

Meg walked on silently.

"We could go to France," she said at last.

"Fat chance," said Joe. Meg thought some more. He knew she knew they didn't need money. She was just looking for an excuse to use that ring again.

"We could buy Aunt Louise a nice present," she

said virtuously. Joe was silent in his turn. He didn't
know what to buy Aunt Louise, but he supposed it
would be a good thing to do. To show that they
knew she couldn't help living in such an awful place
and it wasn't her fault they were having such a boring time.

"How would we earn any money?" he asked, even
though he knew what was coming.

"I could get the ring to make you six feet tall
again," said Meg and grinned. "And I could take
you around and charge people to look at you."

"If I went around with you, people could see me
anyway," Joe told her. "Why would they pay
money?"

"We could go to the playground, and you could
sing and dance," went on Meg. "And those little kids
could throw money at you."

"Those little kids don't have any money," replied
Joe shortly. "And anyway, I wouldn't. Sing and
dance, I mean."

"Well, I'll make me six feet tall and I'll do the
singing and dancing," said Meg.

"You'd probably get arrested," said Joe. Meg
sighed. And then all of a sudden she grabbed Joe's
arm and pinched.

"Listen, Joe, you know what I could do?" she
asked excitedly.

"No, what?" asked Joe sulkily, rubbing his arm. "I'm going to hit you someday when you pinch like that."

"What I could do is," said Meg impressively, "make our feet be like metal detectors. Only not just metal, anything that's valuable. And we could walk around and around until we found something, buried treasure or something, and we could dig it up and sell it. And nobody could tell we did it by magic, it would just be a lucky break. And we might find all kinds of good things."

"No more ring," repeated Joe firmly.

"I'm going to do it," said Meg. "Right after lunch."

"Aw, Meg, there's no treasure around here," said Joe. "That's dumb."

"No, it's not," Meg answered. "Great-Grandfather found all those things in his box right around here— including the ring, I guess. This is an old town, and lots of things have happened here—and maybe one of the things that happened was treasure. And I'm going to do it and you don't have to."

She ran ahead of him. She ran fast and had already washed her hands and eaten half her chili before he got to the lunch table. And his arm still hurt where she'd pinched him. He could see the headlines now: MAJOR LEAGUE PITCHER PERMA-

When lunch was over Aunt Louise went to take
her nap. Before she went upstairs Megan asked if
they might go back to the playground.

"Certainly," answered Aunt Louise. "If you're
careful about crossing the streets. I know I'm being
a nag, but traffic is really awful these days."

She went on up the stairs and Meg waited a few
minutes and then she said, "Come on, Joe. You too,
hear? Because with two of us it doubles the chances
of finding something. And it won't be something
like being little enough to get in the dollhouse that
anybody can see."

Joe thought. He didn't think the ring would do it
in the first place, and in the second place, he didn't
think they were going to find anything, so in the end
he said, "Okay."

Meg rubbed the ring widdershins and said nine
times, "I wish that Joe and I could detect treasure
and valuables buried in the earth with our feet."

Joe wondered what their feet were going to do.
Give out clicking noises if they stepped on a di-
amond mine? Or ring like a bell? Or give off sparks?

They went out of the house. Meg shuffled along
without lifting her feet, but Joe just walked natu-
rally.

"You'll miss something," complained Meg.

"You said this magic wouldn't be something other people could see," Joe told her. "If we go around walking the way you're doing now, everybody can see and everybody's going to think we're crazy. Especially Aunt Louise."

Even Meg could understand that, so she quit shuffling and took little bitty steps, which was almost as bad.

They walked down the sidewalk and Joe said, "It's not going to do you much good to find any treasure here. It's all sidewalk and paving. You'd need a jackhammer to get at it."

"I know," said Meg. "Let's go to Barnard Park."

Barnard Park was a handkerchief-sized park given to the city by a man named Barnard in honor of his parents or his wife or somebody. Aunt Louise had once taken Meg and Joe there. It had three trees and eight bushes and a bench and a dirty little fishpond with mosquito wrigglers in it. Aunt Louise had said Mr. Barnard meant well and it was the only greenery for blocks.

Joe had to admit Barnard Park wasn't paved over. It was bare earth covered with a smatter of grass and weeds. And it was sort of on the way to the playground. So he followed along.

Since it was early summer, Barnard Park looked

almost decent. The leaves of the trees and shrubs were still fresh, the grass was as nearly green as it ever would be, and someone had cleaned out the fishpond. It still didn't have any fish in it.

A man and a woman were sitting on the bench. Meg was furious. She and Joe walked over and looked into the clean and empty fishpond and Joe wondered if she planned to throw up in it. Maybe that would drive the grown people away.

But after a few minutes the woman stood up and said loudly, "I still think seventy dollars is too much to pay for a pair of shoes, even if they are pink!" She walked away angrily, and in a minute the man got up and followed. Joe was really relieved.

"Now," said Meg happily, and she began to shuffle back and forth over the grass.

"You, too," she said over her shoulder to Joe.

He began to walk around, pretending to look at the shrubs and the trunks of the trees. He hoped nobody was watching. He didn't know which of them looked stranger—Meg, scuffing her feet like she was walking on half-chewed bubble gum, or he, walking back and forth between two dumb bushes and staring like he'd just got off a flying saucer from outer space and thought the bushes were senators or something.

No one seemed to notice. He thought it was the

dumbest thing he'd ever done. He hoped Meg got tired of it pretty quick.

Just then the woman who was angry about the seventy-dollar pink shoes came back and sat down on the bench again. Meg and Joe both stopped dead still. The woman didn't pay any attention to them. They waited right where they were, and Meg began to turn faintly green.

Joe looked around wildly. He didn't know what to do. If she threw up, he was going to claim he'd never seen her before in his life.

"Hey, Meg," he called. "Here's a four-leaf clover!"

It wasn't really, it was a clover with three leaves, but one of them had split, so it looked like four.

Meg quit turning green and walked toward him. He watched her anxiously. And all of a sudden he thought she'd seen a snake. She jumped a foot and her eyes got big and she turned bright red, a thing he hadn't often see her do before. He waited for something dire to happen.

Instead she stood quite still except that her right foot moved slowly back and forth over the ground. And then she grinned.

"Treasure!" she said suddenly, just making the shapes of the words with her mouth. "I've found it!"

Joe stood there looking at her for a second before he went over to where she was. Fortunately two of the bushes were between her and the bench so that even if the angry woman had turned around, she wouldn't have been able to see Meg with her right foot pawing the grass like a half-witted pony.

"Here," said Meg softly. "Put your foot right here. Can't you feel it?"

Joe put his foot right there. Did he feel something, like pins and needles, as though his foot had gone to sleep? He wasn't sure.

"What does it feel like?" he asked.

"Like treasure," said Meg briefly.

He put his foot back on the spot and was almost sure he couldn't feel anything. Almost.

They went on looking at each other and stepping on and off that one spot of earth. Joe figured if anybody noticed them, they'd think they were just two dumb kids playing some kind of dumb game.

"What are you going to do?" he asked.

"Dig it up," said Meg. The angry woman suddenly rose from the bench and ran to catch a bus. Her shoes were just ordinary brown shoes. Before she was halfway across the street, Meg was down on her knees, scrabbling away at the dirt.

"I wish we'd had sense enough to bring something to dig with," she panted. "A kitchen spoon or anything."

"Meg, listen," said Joe. "I don't think you're supposed to dig here. This is a public park. I don't think people are supposed to go digging it up."

Meg didn't pay any attention, she just went on digging. But after a minute she said, "I'm getting closer. I really am."

Joe didn't say anything more. It wasn't going to do any good. The bus roared by, and he could see a policeman coming down the street on the side opposite the park.

Meg was going to get arrested. Joe groaned inwardly. He had known from the beginning that that ring was going to get them in real trouble, and now Meg was going to get arrested.

8

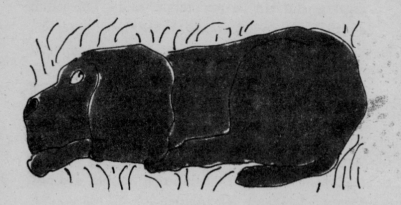

The policeman crossed the street and came toward them.

"Stop digging!" Joe said desperately and got himself between Meg and the officer.

The policeman seemed to be looking right at them. His face was stern. He stepped up onto the sidewalk and Joe said loudly, "Oh, yeah, hello. Could you tell us—er—where—how to get to the Thirty-eighth Street playground?"

The policeman smiled a very nice, friendly smile.

"Sure," he said. "You take a left here at the corner, go four blocks, then take another left and you're right there." He looked at Joe thoughtfully. "But Thirty-eighth Street is really for little kids. You oughta go to Municipal Park. Lots more to do there. Take the North Banner bus and ask the driver where to get off. You can't take that dog on the bus, though. Too big."

Joe didn't ask what dog. Meg had magicked herself into a dog while he wasn't looking. He knew she had. It was one way to keep from getting arrested, although the policeman must not have noticed what she was doing.

Now he went on down the street, and Joe turned around. There was Meg sitting flat on the ground, and a dog was sitting flat on the place where she had been digging.

"He won't get up," said Meg sullenly. "He's sitting on the treasure and he won't get up."

"Meg, that dog probably saved you from going to jail," Joe told her.

He stared at the dog. It was black and the size of a piano, with a sad, kind face. The sort of dog who went around saving people who got shipwrecked or lost in snow storms. Not a St. Bernard but close to, Joe thought.

Meg gave the dog a shove. The dog gave Meg a reproachful look.

"Get up, you old dog!" she cried. And then sud-

67

denly she held up her hand and began to rub the ring. "I wish to be strong enough to pick up this dog," she recited. "I wish to be strong—"

"Meg, for pete's sake!" exclaimed Joe. "There are people all around here. If they saw you pick up a two-ton dog, they'd really freak out."

"I don't care," said Meg. "I want my treasure. I found it, and I want it."

"He's bound to get up sometime or other," Joe pointed out. "We'll just have to wait."

The dog lolled out its huge tongue and stretched itself out, closing its eyes and resting its bucket-sized head on its paws. It seemed to be enjoying the sunshine.

"Get up, you old dog!" Meg repeated. Joe thought hard.

"Listen, Meg," he said after a minute. "Why don't you make it so you can talk dog? I mean, wish that when you say, 'Get up,' he'll understand what you're saying and do it. He looks like a real nice dog. He just doesn't understand about how he's sitting on your treasure."

Meg looked pleased. She rubbed the ring nine times, and nine times over she said, "I wish to be able to make this dog understand me and do what I want him to."

At the end she leaned over and scratched the

dog's head. Finally it opened its eyes.

"Listen, dog," explained Meg. "There's something buried under you and I would like to have it. So will you please get up long enough for me to dig it up?"

Joe was glad she was so polite. Also he was surprised that Meg spoke just plain English. He'd been a little bit scared that she might bark and growl, in which case he might have had to go off and leave her.

After a minute or so, the dog sighed heavily and rolled over and got to its feet. There was the shallow hole Meg had scrabbled in the sooty earth of Barnard Park. Joe had an idea. A good idea.

"Ask him to dig up the treasure for you," he told Meg. Probably dogs couldn't get arrested for digging. And after all, it wasn't their dog. They couldn't be responsible even if it decided to dig up half the town.

"Okay," agreed Meg. "Dog, please dig up the treasure that is buried here."

Obediently the dog scraped with its feet and snuffled with its nose in the hole. By and by, something gleamed faintly in the loose dirt.

"Treasure," breathed Meg. "There it is. Oh, thank you, dog. That's enough digging. You might bust it or something."

She reached into the hole and brushed away the earth and pulled out a small, worn, dark object.

"Good grief," said Meg. "That's not a treasure. It must still be in there."

She put her foot down in the hole and Joe could tell from the look on her face that what she held in her hand was the treasure. He could tell her foot wasn't feeling anything.

"Here," he said. "Let's see it. What is it?"

It was a purse, an old-fashioned, long leather purse with a rusty metal frame and a clasp closing.

"It doesn't even have anything in it," she said disgustedly.

"How can you tell?" asked Joe. "You haven't even looked inside."

The clasp was rusted together. He couldn't open it. But the leather was rubbed and worn and rotted through in several places.

"Hey, Meg, there *is* something in it," Joe cried. "I can feel it!"

He pulled at the crumbling stuff and something slid into his hand. Two small coins of tarnished silver. Two dimes.

"Twenty cents!" yelled Meg. "Some treasure."

"They're old," Joe told her. "Real old." He squinted and squinted and finally read out the dates, very slowly. "One-eight-five-four," he said. "That's way over a hundred years old."

Meg wasn't paying any attention.

"Let's go back to Aunt Louise's," she said after a while. She sounded like she might cry.

They walked home in silence. Joe did feel sorry for her. Anybody who planned on a nursery fender, whatever that was, made of pure gold, and then came up with two dimes had a right to be disappointed, he supposed. But she ought to have learned about that old ring by now.

And then, when they got home, Aunt Louise was gone and the house was locked. They sat on the front porch and stared out at the treeless little square lawn and the straight concrete sidewalk with the hot sun blazing down on it. Joe was terribly thirsty. There was a small hydrant at the side of the house, and he walked over and turned it on and drank. But the water was warm and tasted funny, and he was thirstier than ever when he got through drinking.

He went back up on the porch and wondered if he looked as miserable as Meg did. He was certainly amazed she hadn't thrown up. He wondered where Aunt Louise was and when she would be back.

"Listen, Meg," he said. "Those dimes are tarnished, but they're not worn or bent or anything. Old coins are worth a lot of money sometimes."

"Like how much?" asked Meg.

Joe hadn't the slightest idea. "Fifty dollars," he

said, hoping he sounded like he knew.

"Fifty dollars isn't treasure," Meg told him gloomily. "Treasure is a thousand dollars at least. Or emeralds and diamonds. Or gold."

Joe thought fifty dollars was a lot of money. It would certainly buy Aunt Louise an awfully nice present, with some left over. He was about to say so when he heard footsteps. He turned to look, hoping to see Aunt Louise. But it wasn't Aunt Louise, it was Mrs. Hollowell.

She walked to the bottom of the front steps and looked accusingly at Meg and Joe.

"Your dog," she said, "is in my backyard eating my petunias."

"We don't have a dog," said Joe in surprise.

"He followed you home," Mrs. Hollowell told him. "I saw him. A big black dog."

"Oh," said Joe. "That dog. He's not our dog. We didn't even know he had come with us."

"Well, he's eating my petunias," Mrs. Hollowell repeated. She gave them another unfriendly look and turned around and went back to her house. Joe watched her.

"Meg," he said, "we got to go tell that dog to go home. Mrs. Hollowell might call the dogcatcher. And you can talk to him. And he did dig up the treas—the dimes for you."

"Okay," said Meg in a bored voice.

They went over into Mrs. Hollowell's yard and walked around the house, past the mysterious lump in the side yard. Behind the house Mrs. Hollowell had a row of sad petunias next to her garage. And there was the big black dog. And it really was eating the flowers. A small pink-and-white-striped petal stuck out of its mouth like a tongue. It looked very strange.

"Okay, dog," Meg told him. "You better get out of here and go home, if you know what's good for you. Mrs. Hollowell is probably going to call the dogcatcher if you hang around here eating petunias."

The dog stared at her a minute and then walked slowly down the driveway. Its head and tail drooped, and Joe thought it looked miserable too. They watched it go and then walked back the way they had come.

"I wonder why he likes petunias," said Meg.

"Maybe they're full of vitamins," Joe answered. And then he said, "Oh, gulp!"

Meg looked at him. He hoped he hadn't turned bright red.

"I—I almost f-fell down," he stammered. "I tripped over that hump."

Meg walked on, and it was probably a good thing she was so busy sulking. Because he hadn't stum-

73

bled. He had stepped on top of that hump and it had been like stepping on a live wire. Pins and needles had shot through his foot and clean up his shin. It had been all he could do not to yell. There really was treasure buried there, something important, something neat.

But they couldn't dig it up, not right there in broad daylight in the Hollowells' side yard. And anyway, Joe had this funny feeling that whatever the find was it was meant for him, not Megan. It was something important for him, and she needn't know about it. He wouldn't tell her about it.

Not yet anyway.

Maybe not ever. But how in the world was he going to find out what it was?

When they got back to the house, Aunt Louise was just unlocking the door. She'd had her hair cut at last.

"Hello," she said. "I'm glad you didn't have to wait for me. They called from the beauty shop and said if I came right away, I could get my hair done. And I meant to leave a note in case you got back before me, but I forgot. Oh, it is terribly hot, isn't it? And heavy. No doubt we'll soon have a rain. Let's have something cool to drink."

For once Joe was glad to sit in Aunt Louise's little, rather dark living room. Maybe she wouldn't notice how sulky Meg looked. And how excited Joe looked.

During supper Aunt Louise asked what they had done at the playground.

"We found two old dimes," said Meg unexpectedly. Joe didn't think she'd been listening. She dug them out of her pocket and showed them to her aunt.

"How very curious," said Aunt Louise. "They truly are old. And I expect whoever lost them lost quite a treasure."

Joe jumped. "Twenty cents went a long way in those days," she added.

Oh, said Joe to himself.

"We met a dog," he said quickly. "A big, big black dog. Like a St. Bernard."

"A Newfoundland perhaps," suggested Aunt Louise. "I've often thought of having a dog. But I wouldn't want such a big one. Not in town." She paused and then went on. "Or maybe a cat. A cat would probably be better. But my friend Edith had such a sad experience with a cat."

Joe looked at Meg. Was she listening? Would she bawl and squall if the cat had died? Should he stop Aunt Louise? It was too late.

"She had taken the cat to the vet for his shots," Aunt Louise proceeded. "And she didn't have a cat carrier, so she tied him up in a pillowcase. And when she got to the vet's and opened the door to get him, he tumbled out of the front seat, still in his pillowcase, and went tumbling around the sidewalk like a lot of live laundry. Many people were frightened and one woman fainted and broke her arm when she fell."

Aunt Louise shook her head regretfully. It was bad to break your arm, Joe thought. But it must have been funny to see an animated pillowcase rolling along the sidewalk.

"So Edith gave him to her nephew," finished Aunt Louise. "Perhaps I'd better not have a cat." And she began to clear the table.

While they were eating supper the rain had begun. Joe heard it softly falling outside the windows, and then harder and harder, with thunder and lightning. He wondered if he dared get up in the night and dig up whatever that was. The rain would make digging easier.

Could he do it? Was it illegal to dig up someone else's yard? He was sure it was, even if he put the dirt and grass back very carefully. He supposed if the Hollowells wanted to bury a lot of gold and diamonds under their dining-room windows it was their business. And people ought to leave them alone.

But whatever was buried there wasn't gold and

diamonds, he thought. It was something meant for him, something important for him. He knew it, the way Meg had known that old washer was a magic ring. He had to think of a way to get it. He just had to.

He went to bed early and turned off his light and lay awake, listening to the rain and thinking and thinking. There had to be a way.

9

It was still raining hard next morning. Joe felt awful. He'd been awake half the night. And Meg came into his room while he was still asleep and woke him by pinching his arm really hard.

"Meg, you pinch me like that again and I'm going to clobber you," he said crossly.

"Well, Aunt Louise said to wake you up, and that's the best way," Meg answered and went out of the room.

It was going to be a terrible day, Joe could tell. The rain made everything worse. Probably something dire was going to happen. And one of his socks had a hole in it.

At breakfast Aunt Louise tried very hard to make conversation.

"Once, when I was living in this very house," she said, "the house across the street was struck by lightning. I was about eight years old. I was looking out the window of my room—your room, Meg—when it happened. I was quite terrified."

Joe asked, "Was anybody killed?" Meg helped herself to strawberry preserves.

"Oh, the house was empty at the time," Aunt Louise said. "But it was extensively damaged by fire. And for years after that, whenever there was an electrical storm, I went down in the basement."

The basement! Joe had forgotten about the tidy little basement that you got into through a trapdoor on the back porch. Was there a shovel in the basement, or even a trowel? He stared hard at Aunt Louise while he pondered this question, and she said finally, "I was a very nervous child. Many things frightened me then."

Joe was embarrassed. "I guess that would scare anybody," he mumbled and ate his bacon.

"I used to be scared of rats," said Meg. "But I got over it."

There was a long silence. At last Aunt Louise asked if anyone wanted more biscuits. No one did. The rain poured down.

"Perhaps the weather will clear up this afternoon," suggested Aunt Louise. Joe and Meg did not respond. Anybody could tell it was going to rain all day and probably tomorrow.

When they had tidied up from breakfast, Joe went upstairs and sat on his bed and thought hard. If there was a trowel in the basement, he could get it and sneak out of the house after dark. The ground would be soft . . . he wouldn't take what was buried under that hump. He'd just look at it to see what it was and then put it back. He only wanted to know what it was that was so important.

Anyway, probably the Hollowells had thrown it away, whatever it was. Surely, if you really wanted something, you didn't stick it in some old hole in the ground. Unless you had stolen it. And in that case, it ought to be dug up and returned to its rightful owner, thought Joe virtuously. So he'd be doing a good thing if he could only think how to do it.

He got up and stared out the window at the rain. Was it ever going to stop? Maybe he could think of a reason for going to a hardware store. But he guessed he couldn't, and he probably didn't have enough money to buy a trowel. How much did trowels cost? Five dollars? Twenty cents?

Meg came into his room and took his place on the bed. She pulled her hair over her ear for a long time, and at last she said, "I know there's treasure here somewhere. I wish it would stop raining."

"Listen, Meg," explained Joe patiently. "There's a lot of this town. You couldn't walk all over it trying to find any old treasure if you had a year to do it in. Not over every bit of it. And anyway, it's not going to stop raining. Not for a long time anyway."

"I wish I was two people," said Meg in a discontented voice. "If I was two people I could walk twice as much. And one of me could be out walking while the other one was here eating lunch. Aunt Louise would never know."

She looked at Joe, and all at once she got so pale Joe could almost see through her. She held up her hand and began to rub the ring. "I wish I was two people, I wish I was two people . . . ," she whispered hurriedly, and suddenly she was. Two Megs sitting pale and wide-eyed on Joe's bed.

Gosh, he thought. Things could've been a lot worse. Meg could've been twins.

"Am I?" she whispered, only both Megs whispered. "Am I two people?"

The voices were exactly the same, speaking at exactly the same time, so that it was like one voice, only different, weird and echo-y and awful.

"See for yourself," answered Joe. She turned her head, both heads turned, and then whipped around again at once.

"Ugh," said both Megs. "Oh, ugh, that was horrible!"

"Why?" asked Joe in spite of himself. It was all horrible as far as he was concerned.

"Oh, it's like mirrors and mirrors," the Megs quavered. Joe could understand what she meant. When the real Meg turned her head to the right, she could see the false Meg, and the false Meg turning her head to the right could see another Meg, and so on and so on. And the real Meg could see them all because she was both of them. Or at least Joe thought that was the way it must be.

Both the Megs stood up, moving in perfect unison. Joe turned his head so he didn't have to look at them.

"Cut it out," he ordered. "It isn't going to work. And it's creepy. Cut it out, Meg."

The two Megs went to look at themselves in Joe's mirror. And then they sighed.

"Rats," they said. "That isn't what I meant. I guess I'll have to undo it."

I just hope she can, thought Joe and watched while both of them rubbed the ring nine times and said, "I wish to be one person again." It was the weirdest thing he'd ever seen, and he was relieved when there was only one Meg again. He didn't trust that ring. Just any minute now Meg was going to do something with it that she couldn't undo. Or that would get her arrested.

Meg wandered around the room, and Joe started to ask her to go away. He wanted to think. But he didn't dare ask her. She'd be suspicious. And one thing he had definitely decided and was sure of: that it was his treasure and he was going to get it all by himself, without Meg and that ring. Somehow.

They got out the box of Great-Grandfather's keepsakes and looked through them once more. Joe looked because there wasn't anything else to do, and Meg looked hoping that something else magic would turn up. Nothing did.

"Aunt Louise says a nursery is a sort of playroom for little kids," Meg told him suddenly. "In England. Or used to be. And a fender is a sort of metal thing they put in front of the fire to keep it from popping out on the floor and burning the house down."

"Oh," said Joe. He could think of a lot better things to turn into gold than a nursery fender. Still, he supposed it would do if it was right there.

"If I swallow this marble, maybe it would make me invisible," she went on dreamily.

"Maybe it would make you have to go to a doctor," Joe answered. He watched her warily, but she put the marble down. He didn't want to have to remind her about Ken Garbin's dog who'd died when it swallowed an acorn. If she thought of it, she'd cry, more than likely.

He picked up the marble and looked at it a long time. If he was invisible it would be easy to sneak out and dig up whatever that was. Oh, well, if he went out at night he'd be nearly invisible anyway. . . .

When he was putting away the pancake turner after lunch, Joe tried to get a good look at all the cooking things. Were any of the spoons strong enough to dig with? He guessed they would do, the biggest ones. After dark, he could come down and get one maybe.

He tried and tried to think of a reason for asking Aunt Louise to let him go down into the basement. He tried to stop thinking about the whole thing. He had to find some way to get out of the house and dig up that hump of earth, and he would do it. But right now, thinking about it just seemed to make things more dismal.

Aunt Louise went to take her nap. Meg and Joe stayed in the living room, which was darker than ever because of the rain. Meg took out the ring and wished she were an Indian snake charmer. The ring wouldn't do it, so then she wished she had lots of black hair again. And she did.

"I look great," she said, admiring herself in a little mirror over the couch.

"I think you look awful," said Joe. "Anyway,

you're going to wear that ring out making it do dumb things like that, Meg."

"No, I won't," she said quickly. "Magic doesn't wear out. At least not often. I mean, if you got three wishes, then when your three wishes had been granted that would be the end of that. But a magic ring doesn't wear out or run down or anything."

"Well, you said it might get mad," Joe pointed out. "It looks like it would make it mad to be always giving you a lot of dumb hair that looks awful on you anyway."

Meg sighed and wished back her own wispy reddish-brown hair.

"I wish I could wish it would stop raining," she said. "Oh, look, it is stopping, Joe!"

Joe looked. The rain had died to a drizzle, but it was still coming down and would be for some time. And they couldn't go out in it. Still, maybe by ten o'clock it would have stopped, and that would make things easier, he told himself.

"Oh, why doesn't something exciting happen?" complained Meg. "I mean something different—like when we could breathe underwater. Or if we could make a little volcano come up in Aunt Louise's front yard and have an eruption. Just a little one with just a little lava and just a little bit of sparks flying around."

That would be fun, Joe had to admit. Meg was nuts, but he wouldn't mind seeing something like that.

"Or a plague of snakes out in the street—or—or —somebody coming to deliver a great big color TV to Aunt Louise," she continued. And then all at once she looked wicked, really wicked.

Oh, gosh, something dire is going to happen, thought Joe. But nothing happened. Meg moved over to the window and stood looking out. He couldn't see her face any more and didn't know whether she was planning on fainting or throwing up. Or what.

And then, after five minutes which seemed like forever, it happened. There was a growl under the window and then another, and then the sound of various running paws. He jumped over to the window and looked out.

Aunt Louise's tiny yard and the Hollowells' and the sidewalk and street, everywhere, was crowded with dogs. The big black dog was there, and collies and terriers and sheepdogs and a bulldog with a sweet smashed face and plain dogs of all sizes and colors and shapes. A sea of dogs, of brown and black and white spotted backs, of curled and shaggy and smooth and plumy tails.

They weren't doing anything much, just trotting around, sniffing the wet earth and the sooty hedges and sidewalks. Once in a while one or another would growl or snap, but not often. It was a strange sight. Joe hadn't known there were that many dogs in the whole town.

"How'd you do it?" he asked Meg cautiously.

She grinned. "I got the ring to let me whistle like one of those dog whistles nobody but dogs can hear," she said. "And to make it so all the dogs that heard had to come here."

"Okay," he said. "But you better hurry up and think of some way to make them go away. Because you're going to make the dogcatcher and the police and a lot of newspaper reporters come too, I bet."

Already doors were opening up and down the street and heads were peering nervously out of windows.

"Oh, that'll be easy," Meg answered airily. "I'll just go tell that big black dog to tell the others to get going."

"Well, how are you going to get to him?" Joe wanted to know. For the big black dog was across the street and there was a whole river of dogs between Meg and him. Joe didn't see why the ring wouldn't let Meg be an Indian snake charmer and then would let her pull a stunt like this. He supposed nobody would ever guess she was responsible. How could they?

"Look, you got to get rid of them quick," he muttered. "They're all going to get run over, if nothing else. Come on."

They went out on the porch, and a pleasant-looking little brown-and-white dog ran up the steps to meet them. It was scary to walk down the steps right into the middle of ten thousand dogs, Joe thought. Well, a thousand anyway. More dogs than he had ever seen in one place before in his life.

"Get out of the way," Meg said to several terriers. But there was really nowhere much for them to get. She stepped over one and squeezed past a big hound of some sort with sad eyes and sad ears.

"Get a move on, Meg," urged Joe. "There's a truck coming this way."

The truck was a block away, inching slowly forward among the dogs. And there was a car behind it.

It didn't take long to cross the street, but it seemed forever to Joe. A woman shouted at them to go back, and someone else yelled something about the police. The dogs panted and barked, getting more and more excited and louder and louder.

Joe hoped the big black dog would stay where it was. A dog that size could go wherever it wanted to. It was bigger than any of the others.

Meg and that ring were both nuts. Suppose that black dog hadn't turned up? How would they have gotten rid of all these others? Joe asked himself.

But the dog was still standing in the yard across the street, looking kind and noble and huge, with lots of smaller dogs milling and shoving around it.

"Come here, big dog," called Meg. And it came, stepping on a poodle as it went. The poodle looked offended. Meg put her hand on the dog's head.

"Tell them all to go home quick," she told it. "Before the dogcatcher comes. I won't whistle again."

The black dog gazed at her for a moment rather reproachfully as though it had expected something else. Joe wondered if maybe the dogs had been bored too and had come when Meg whistled, thinking something great was going to happen. A lot of bones to bury or rabbits to chase. And now they were going to have to go home.

Still, it must have been sort of exciting for them. Joe didn't believe any of these dogs had ever seen this many dogs together before either.

The big dog turned away. It nipped at a beagle and barked once—and the dogs began to leave. Slowly they wandered off, in one direction or another. The woman who had yelled at Meg and Joe to go home came down her steps and cried, "Scat!" at two terriers.

"Did you ever see anything like that?" she called to her neighbor. "What do you suppose made them come here? And what made them leave?"

"Come on, Meg," said Joe hurriedly. He didn't want the neighbors to have a chance to start noticing Meg and how she had talked to the black dog.

They crossed back to their side of the street. One dog, a small, plain, busy little light-brown dog, still lingered in the Hollowells' yard. And this dog wasn't leaving. It was industriously digging up the mysterious hump in the Hollowells' side yard!

Mud was flying, the dog was burrowing frantically. It was digging up whatever it was that belonged to Joe.

"Hey, quit that!" he yelled without thinking. "Go on home!"

"Oh, for pete's sake," said Meg. "It's not hurting anything."

"Yes, it is," said Joe. "We got to make it quit. You ought to, Meg. You brought those dogs here and you ought not to let 'em make holes in people's yards."

He ran over to the hedge and yelled again, "Go

on home!" The little dog looked up curiously from its digging. Joe yelled and waved his arms and after a minute it gave one more scrabble with its brown paws and then trotted away.

There was a really deep hole. Joe longed to go over and look in, but he was scared to. He was worried to death about whatever it was in there that was meant for him, but he didn't say anything because he still didn't want Meg to know anything about it. He followed her into the house, and Aunt Louise came hurrying down the stairs.

"What were you children doing out in the wet?" she asked anxiously. "What was all that yelling about? Are you all right?"

"There were a lot of dogs in the front yard," explained Joe in a hurry. "We went out to run them off."

"That was thoughtful," replied Aunt Louise. "Odd, I didn't know there were many dogs in the neighborhood. Do go change your shirts, you look thoroughly drenched."

Joe took off his T-shirt and found another in a drawer. He wished he had Meg's room instead of this one. Meg's window was right over the roof of the porch. Maybe he could climb out on the roof and get down from it and go over to the Hollowells' without anyone noticing. Rats! He had to think of something.

The afternoon wore on.

The mail came. There was a postcard, showing the Eiffel Tower, from Mother. "Having a wonderful time," it said. "Love, Mother and Daddy." Not even "Wish you were here."

"She might have said, 'Wish you were here,' " Meg pointed out huffily.

"I guess she doesn't," Joe said. "I mean, like you wouldn't want Mother and Daddy along if you were going to camp, would you?"

"It's not the same thing," said Meg, but she knew it was.

She got a book and began to read.

Joe and Aunt Louise played two games of Chinese checkers. Joe won. He didn't know how. He wasn't even thinking much about what he was doing, but his marbles seemed to get in the right places somehow. He was surprised. He wasn't good at that kind of game usually.

Aunt Louise went out to the kitchen to do something about supper, she said. The rain drizzled down. The sky was dark, and the clouds still hung low over the street. Meg turned a page in her book and the clock ticked. Suddenly Joe couldn't bear it another minute.

He stood up, and Meg just went on reading. He went out of the living room into the hall, and still she didn't pay any attention. He unlocked the screen door quietly and opened it carefully. He didn't think it squeaked. None of Aunt Louise's doors squeaked. He stood on the front porch waiting for Meg to holler at him or come after him wanting to know what he was doing. Nothing happened. He held his breath.

And then softly he made his way across the porch and down the steps and into the little front yard. The ground was squishy underfoot. There was no one in sight in the damp twilight. Joe stepped over the hedge into the Hollowells' yard and walked up to the hole which only a few hours ago had been a mysterious bump. He peered in. What was there?

Could the dog have been after the same thing he, Joe, was after? And what could be so important to Joe that a dog would want? That wasn't what he meant. He meant, what could a dog want that would be so important to a boy like him, who just wanted to be the world's greatest baseball pitcher? He knelt and put his hand down in the hole—and found some rocks. A lot of small rocks piled up and buried. That's all that mysterious hump was—rocks.

His hand moved here and there and closed over one of them, a flat, smooth, slick-feeling piece of stone. It was his treasure! He knew at once. It was almost alive in his hand, even his fingers could tell it was important.

His heart bumped, and he crouched there, stroking the rock gently and trying to get the mud off. It was engraved or something. He could feel tiny lines and shallow pits all along it.

He tried rubbing the mud off on the grass, and then he remembered some grubby Kleenex in his pocket and he used that. It was hard to see in the dim light, and he stood up and moved away from the house where the light was better.

And then he knew what it was. A fossil! A single long, graceful fern frond that had been pressed into the mud a million years ago, a billion years ago. And now it was here in Joe's hand, and it felt strange, cold and hard and sleek and yet somehow— alive.

It was the only way Joe could think of it. It felt so alive it almost seemed to move, and he thought he could feel pins and needles in his palm the way he had in his foot when he had stepped on the hump.

Why hadn't he known before that fossils were the most important thing in the world? Way more important than baseball, or even being sixteen and having a driver's license and learning to drive a car. He stood there, staring at the stone and thinking about it, and he nearly jumped out of his skin when Meg walked up to him and said, "What's that?"

"Just a rock," he answered, holding it out so that the fossil didn't show. It wasn't that he didn't want her to know about the fossil. But he wanted a chance to look at it more carefully all by himself. It was his, and he wanted to be the first one to see it clearly.

"Then why were you looking at it like that?" she demanded. "Why are you out here in the rain staring at some old rock like it—like it was a chocolate soda?"

"I wasn't," Joe began, and she interrupted, "Where'd you get it?"

"Over there," he told her, pointing at the hole. She drew in her breath.

"It's treasure, isn't it?" she asked loudly. "You felt it with your feet, didn't you? This afternoon with the dog when it was eating petunias?"

"It's just a rock," Joe said again, but she wasn't listening. "And you went and got it all by yourself, didn't you?" she yelled. "That was mean. You wouldn't have found it without me and the ring. That was mean, Joe."

"Be quiet, would you, Meg?" he pleaded. "Everybody in town can hear you."

"I bet you didn't get the real treasure," she cried. "I bet there's still things in there."

She ran over to the hole and squatted and began to pull out rocks.

"Hey, look, Meg," he called. "It's a fossil. You can have it if you want. Come on away from there."

Meg went on scooping out the muddy rocks, and after a minute she said, "Okay for you, Joe, I'm not going to show you what I find either."

He didn't know what to do. Mr. Hollowell was bound to come out and yell at them, or worse. Joe stood there in the fading light, holding his fossil and feeling dumb.

And then Meg called, "I found it! I found it! And it isn't any old fossil either."

She stood up, and something gleamed in her fingers, something green and gold and valuable-looking. And she was standing there with it in her hand when a policeman walked around the corner of the house.

Joe was scared. He wanted to run, but he knew it wouldn't do any good, and anyway he couldn't. His legs wouldn't move. It was his fault. He should have waited till after dark to go look for his treasure. The policeman walked straight up to Meg, and Mr. Hollowell was right behind him.

"What's going on?" asked the policeman, and Mr. Hollowell said loudly, "Rotten kids! Vandals! Digging up my lawn. Hard enough to get a little grass growing here anyway. . . ."

Megan stared at the policeman. She didn't even have the good sense to shut her hand, Joe thought, and whatever it was she had found lay there on her palm, looking more and more gold and valuable. And Mr. Hollowell let out a yell, "My wife's antique brooch! My wife's brooch! They've stolen my wife's brooch too," he bawled at the officer.

And then he hollered up at the dining-room window, "Amelia, come out here! Right now."

Nobody else said anything, they just stood there. Oh, why didn't Meg use the ring? Joe asked himself. She could magic them down to the size of peas, and they could roll down in the gutter and nobody need ever hear of them again. A pigeon could eat them, or they could drown in a beer can.

Mrs. Hollowell came hurrying up. She wore a man's old bathrobe clutched around her, and in her left hand she carried an umbrella, although it wasn't raining any more. She looked at Joe, and then she looked at Meg and the policeman, and then she looked at the hole.

"Oh, George," she said faintly. "I know you said not to. But I couldn't just put him in the garbage. I knew it was illegal. I knew I'd be arrested."

Her voice trembled and she began to cry.

"What do you mean?" asked Mr. Hollowell sharply. And Mrs. Hollowell dropped the umbrella and put her hands up to her mouth while the tears rolled down. In a muffled voice she said, "Officer, arrest me. I knew it was wrong. I couldn't help it, though. I had to do it."

"Do what, Amelia?" roared Mr. Hollowell.

And Mrs. Hollowell answered, "That hole. It's where I buried Richard."

And it was then that Meg fainted.

11

They all sat around Aunt Louise's kitchen table, even the policeman. The policeman was very big and he looked uncomfortable in Aunt Louise's tiny kitchen.

They were all eating chicken salad sandwiches and ham and drinking various things. No matter what anyone wanted, Aunt Louise managed to produce it. Almost like magic.

Joe was having chocolate milk. Meg wasn't eating, which Joe thought was probably a good thing. She looked definitely green, and he wanted to go on enjoying his chicken salad sandwich and not have to watch her throwing up hers.

Joe admired Aunt Louise. She hadn't seemed in the least disturbed when she came out and saw Meg, covered with mud and very white-faced and looking dead as she lay on the ground, and the policeman and Mrs. Hollowell in her bathrobe still crying and the umbrella rolling down the sidewalk.

Aunt Louise had simply got Meg up on her feet and told everyone to come into her kitchen. She made Meg and Joe wash off the mud and sat everyone around the kitchen table and spread out the food, quite calmly, as though she had expected all these people to come to supper and act in such a weird way.

Mrs. Hollowell dabbed at her eyes.

"George told me it was illegal," she said once more. Aunt Louise laid her hand gently on Mrs. Hollowell's arm.

"What was illegal?" she asked kindly. "I'm sure it wasn't anything very bad. Please tell us exactly what happened."

The policeman helped himself to more ham.

"Well, we had had Richard for twelve years," she began and sniffed deeply.

"Her poodle," put in Mr. Hollowell.

"A toy poodle," explained Mrs. Hollowell. "Such a dear little dog. So intelligent." More tears gathered in her eyes, but she went on bravely. "The vet said his heart was bad and he might go at any time."

Joe hoped Meg wasn't going to howl.

"And I picked out a spot in the yard where I planned to bury him," Mrs. Hollowell said. "And then George told me it was illegal. Inside the city limits you are not allowed to bury animals in your yard."

The policeman nodded. "Sanitation regulations," he mumbled from behind his sandwich.

"George said," Mrs. Hollowell continued, "to put his body in a plastic sack and put it in the garbage."

Meg howled. It was better than throwing up, but it was awful enough. It took a while to get her to shut up and let Mrs. Hollowell tell what happened next.

"We went out to Thanksgiving dinner last November," she said. "We don't often go out, but George's cousin asked us, so we went. And we got home long after dark—and poor little Richard was dead. He'd just slipped away in his sleep."

Aunt Louise looked firmly at Meg, who howled silently. Mrs. Hollowell wiped her eyes.

"I got out a plastic bag—and then—and then—I looked at him and he was so tiny and I couldn't bear the thought of him in a garbage truck. It was a nice, mild night so, well, I slipped outside and got a spade and buried him there under the dining-room windows."

"Over there." Mr. Hollowell pointed through the kitchen window. Joe didn't see why, they all knew.

"Our son Edwin had had a rock collection when he was young and the rocks were still in the basement," Mrs. Hollowell said, "and I spread some over Richard's body, to keep other dogs from digging him up, you know. And I buried him. And I knew it was wrong."

She began to cry again. Joe put his hand in his pocket and touched his fossil. It had once belonged to Edwin Hollowell. But Edwin must not want it any more. And now it was Joe's. Still, Joe thought he should tell. If everybody was going to get arrested, he might as well too. So he brought the fossil out and put it on the table.

"This afternoon a dog did try to dig up that grave," he said. "And I went to look in the hole and found this."

No one paid much attention to the fossil.

"What dog?" asked Mr. Hollowell. So Joe explained that some dogs had come into the neighborhood that afternoon. He didn't say how many.

"Several dogs," he said carefully. "One of them came up on Aunt Louise's porch. Megan and I went out and drove them away. But one of them had already dug up the—the grave. I walked—Meg and I walked over a while ago to look in the hole and that's when I found this fossil and Meg found that—that other thing."

The other thing lay on the table. It was made of gold and emeralds, Mr. Hollowell said. It had belonged to Mrs. Hollowell's mother, and it was very valuable. Joe tried not to look at it.

"You see," added Mrs. Hollowell, "I was so upset about Richard, and about doing something that was against the law, it was several days before I thought about the brooch. I looked and looked. I forgot I had worn it to the Thanksgiving party. Oh, dear."

She wiped her nose. "We thought it must have been stolen. We went to the police, at least George did, and we offered a reward. I am very glad to have it back."

There was a long silence. Joe wondered if he dared slip his fossil off the table and back in his pocket. He looked at it longingly. How old was it? What kind of fern was it? What kind of stone had formed out of that long-ago mud?

The policeman wiped his mouth and dropped his paper napkin. He cleared his throat and then took a notebook from his pocket.

"That's Mr. George Hollowell, 2317 Elberton," he began. "You spell that H-o-l-l-o—"

"Well, officer," said Mr. Hollowell hastily. "I don't guess we'll be pressing any charges. After all, it wasn't the kids who dug up the lawn, I suppose."

Joe wondered if Mr. Hollowell had seen Meg crouching by Richard's grave, clawing out the rocks and throwing them in all directions. Maybe not.

"You might say they was trespassing," said the policeman. "But then you'd have to consider that the open hole was what we call an 'attractive nuisance.'"

He looked very pleased with this phrase. Mr. Hollowell looked slightly insulted. Meg and Mrs. Hollowell both sniffed.

"I suppose I am the only one who has done anything really illegal," said Mrs. Hollowell slowly.

"Well, ma'am," said the policeman, "seeing it was such a little dog and such a while ago, I guess we can forget about it. I don't guess you would do it again, now, would you?"

Mrs. Hollowell shook her head, looking sadder and sadder. Aunt Louise stood up and said briskly, "These children really should be getting to bed. They have had a strenuous evening."

"That's right, ma'am," said the policeman, standing up too and looking at the last chicken salad sandwich longingly. Aunt Louise put it in a paper napkin and gave it to him, and in a minute she was gently ushering the policeman and the Hollowells out the front door.

No one had mentioned the fossil. Joe reached out slowly and slipped it into his pocket again. Meg watched.

"Now, Meg," she said when they were gone. "Run take your bath. I'll bring you something to eat on a tray."

Meg went upstairs and Joe followed her. He didn't really have anything else to do, and besides, he wanted to be in his room all by himself and get a really good look at this fossil at last. Meg came right on in with him and crouched on the end of his bed, looking miserable. Looking like she might cry again any minute.

"Meg, you better go take your bath," said Joe. He didn't want to have her bawling all over his bed. "You're still muddy."

"I lost the ring," said Meg wretchedly. "While I was getting the treasure out of the hole."

"Gee," said Joe. "Oh, gee, I'm sorry."

He wasn't really. He'd been right about that ring. It had come very near getting Meg really arrested and maybe him too.

Meg stared into space. After a minute she stood up.

"Oh, well," she said. "That ring couldn't do so much. And I could make it work. I can do real magic. I can do it all by myself. Some day I will,

I know I will!" And then she added smugly, "I made sure of that."

She went out of the room, and in a minute Joe heard the bath water running loudly and lots of splashing. He sat down on the bed and looked at his fossil, at the lovely curved stone fern frond, all its tiny veined leaves and stems turned to reddish smooth stone so long, long ago. He did not hear Aunt Louise until she was right in the room.

"Here, Joe," she said. "Here's something for you. It was my father's book, and it hasn't been opened for years. I suppose it isn't very up-to-date, but I thought you might be interested."

He took the book and opened it politely. Surely by now Aunt Louise must know about how he couldn't read, not really read.

The first word he saw on the page was *Dire*. "Dire wolves were fairly common during the Ice Age," he read. "Other carnivores included the smilodon, a saber-toothed tiger larger and heavier than today's lion. . . ." He turned a few pages. "The exoskeleton is almost like a shell. . . ."

Joe looked up at Aunt Louise, too startled to speak. He could read! He could read hard words like *carnivore* and *exoskeleton* without any trouble at all!

It had happened just the way the reading therapist

had said it would. "Joe doesn't have any real eye disorder," she had told his mother. "It's just that the muscles of his eyes haven't caught up with the rest of him yet. Give him a few years and maybe some eye exercises and he'll be able to read as well as anyone. You'll see. Sometimes it happens almost overnight."

It was true. He hadn't believed it would ever happen, but it had. He could read like mad.

"Gosh, thanks, Aunt Louise," he said at last. "Oh, gosh, thanks. It's a great book."

"I thought you'd like it," she answered.

"Several true ferns appear in late Devonian times . . . ," Joe read. Oh, poor Meg. What was magic compared to the Cambrian and Silurian ages?

The next morning was beautiful and clear and cool. The sky was as blue and cloudless as if rain had never been invented. Meg was glum, and Joe tried hard to think of some way to cheer her up. He told her about mammals like megatherium and glyptodon, but she wasn't very interested.

"I don't see much point in knowing all about animals there aren't any more of," she said finally. Joe saw a lot of point.

"Maybe we ought to go back to that playground," he suggested. He was worried that Meg would take it into her head to find that ring. He didn't think the Hollowells would like her coming over there, and he didn't want to see any more of that ring.

"You go," said Meg. "I don't want to."

And then the telephone rang, and Aunt Louise talked a long time. Joe read and Meg stared at the wall. The telephone was out in the hall, and he could hear Aunt Louise saying something about his mother, but he wasn't really paying attention. And he was surprised when she came in and said, "That was your Aunt Julie."

Julie was Mother's youngest sister. Joe and Meg had wanted to stay with Julie and her husband, Tom, while Mother and Daddy were away. They lived in the country, on almost a farm. They had a pony, and even though their kids were younger than Meg and Joe, they were good kids. They could even play pretty good ball.

But just before Mother had decided to go to France, she'd had a letter from Julie. And the letter said, "We're going to visit Tom's father. He's having a lot of trouble with his eyesight and we may be some time. . . ." So Mother had said she couldn't even suggest that Joe and Meg stay with Julie and her family.

Now Aunt Louise shook her head.

"Julie is going to have to buy a typewriter," she

said. Joe was amazed. Why had Julie called Aunt Louise long distance to say she was going to have to buy a typewriter?

"Oh, it's really ridiculous for a grown woman to have such dreadful handwriting," she went on. "I must admit mine isn't too good, but I try to take some care when I write a letter. Julie just scrawls."

And it turned out that what Julie had written was "We're going to visit Tom's father. He's having a lot of trouble with his chickens and we may bring some back."

They'd only been gone a day, and now Julie was indignant that Mother and Daddy hadn't sent Joe and Meg to stay with them. It was too much to ask of Aunt Louise, and anyway, Julie's farm was a much better place to be than in the city in a hot summer.

So she and Tom would arrive tomorrow and drive the children back with them. Even Meg looked pleased.

12

"Want to put your books back here with the bags?" asked Tom.

"No, thanks," Joe answered. "I'll keep 'em with me. I might read."

"Okay," said Tom and slammed the tailgate.

Joe had two books, his grandfather's and a new book about fossils bought yesterday. He had sat up late reading, really reading. It was far out.

This will be the first trip I ever took when I wasn't bored to bits, Joe thought. When I'll have just as much to think about as Meg. About trilobites and pteropods and ammonoids. About ice ages and tar pits. . . . .

"Good-bye, Aunt Louise," said Meg. "Thank you for everything." Which showed that Meg could really be polite, could really be nice if she wanted to.

"It was great," added Joe. "And the food was good too."

Aunt Louise laughed. "It was lovely having you for a few days," she told them. "Now, Tom, do drive carefully."

They all got in, Meg and Joe in the back and Tom and Julie in the front. Julie said, "You take care too, Aunt Louise," and leaned out the window to kiss her once more. Aunt Louise looked pleased.

"Come again, all of you," she invited. "And I hope the children weren't too bored."

And they drove away.

"You weren't, were you?" asked Julie, fiddling with the air conditioner. "Bored, I mean."

"No," said Meg. "We went to the playground. And we went to see Pat."

Going to see Pat had been fun, Joe thought. There was a lake—and hadn't there been something about the lake he had wanted to tell Daddy and Mother? Something about some big fish? Was that it? Hadn't there been some big fish? Oh, well.

"Mrs. Hollowell almost got arrested," he said. That had been exciting. A policeman had come, he remembered that. But he had come to Aunt Louise's house, not the Hollowells'. Joe wasn't sure why. Some sort of mix-up.

What had Mrs. Hollowell done to get nearly arrested? She had lost something. Was it a ring? That hardly seemed something to make the police nearly arrest her. Anyway, Meg had found whatever Mrs. Hollowell had lost, and Mrs. Hollowell had given Meg a reward. A whole hundred dollars. Joe had never known a kid Meg's age who owned a whole hundred dollars.

"We had a good time," he finished slowly.

Julie turned around to look at them over the back of the seat.

"I didn't think you'd been bored," she said, smiling. "When I was your age and stayed with her a few times, I wasn't bored. I had fun."

"What did you do?" asked Tom.

"Oh, I don't know," replied Julie. "I really can't remember. Isn't that strange? I don't remember. But I had fun. . . ."

Great-Aunt Louise walked into the room which Meg had occupied during the children's visit. Aunt Louise raised the shades to let in the sun, stripped the sheets from the bed, and briskly turned the mattress. And then suddenly she moved over to the windows and held out her hand.

113

"Come hither, my lovely one," she said softly. And there in her palm lay Meg's ring. Only it was no longer dark and dull. It was made of beaten gold, old, old ancient gold, glowing and rosy with age. The marks and scratches showed up plainly as symbols and runes.

Aunt Louise smiled. "Meg did very well with the ring, all things considered," she said aloud. "I know Amelia was very glad to get that all cleared up, about poor Richard. And I'm sure the children didn't have a dull time while they were here."

She was silent a minute, thinking. "I should think everyone would believe in magic," she began again. "Just look at how Joe learned to read. And I had nothing to do with it!" She looked very pleased.

"Yes, taking into account the limitations I put on the ring's powers, Meg did very well. Better than I had expected. In fact, I was truly surprised when she made that last wish. It was rather clever."

She sighed and put the ring in her pocket and pointed at the sheets dumped on the floor. The sheets immediately gathered themselves up into a neat, freshly laundered pile, smelling of lavender and sunshine.

"After all, I'm not getting any younger," she went on. "I should certainly see that some one of my nieces and nephews inherits the ring and knows all my secrets. And I do believe Meg is the proper one. Just as soon as she gets over this golden nursery fender idea. As soon as she learns that magic is for making life pleasant and exciting. Not for making one rich. I shouldn't think she'd take long to learn that."

Now she smiled again. "Yes, Meg shall be the one."

MARY Q. STEELE
has written many popular books for children. Under the pen name of Wilson Gage she is the author of *Squash Pie* and *Down in the Boondocks,* both ALA Notable Books, and *Mrs. Gaddy and the Ghost.* Under her own name she is the author of *Journey Outside,* a Newbery Honor Book, as well as many other books, including *The True Men, The Owl's Kiss,* and *Because of the Sand Witches There.*